Oh, How We Laughed*

A Blue Feet Anthology
by Queer, Disabled South Australians

Curated by Jace Reh and Theo Brown
Edited by Alex Dunkin

---

* Cried, chuckled, suffered, retreated, enjoyed, blanked, masked, cringed, smiled, consumed, planned, protested, disappeared, felt, overthought, withdrew, celebrated, raged, meditated, screamed, froze, danced, existed…

About *Oh, How We Laughed**

Jace Reh and Theo Brown bring together artwork, poetry, and prose from Queer, Disabled South Australians for the anthology, *Oh, How We Laughed**. Creativity and laughter are universal. They aren't a constant but are a strong point of connection. We experience fear, joy, loss, exhilarating highs, depressive lows, and so much more. How we express those emotions might be different or not at all, yet amongst all this we can always strive for a laugh.

The creative works featured in this anthology draw from a wide range of experiences and expressions. They share thoughts through fiction and pure creative forms. They delve into sharp realisations and convey these in direct non-fiction texts. There are pieces that feel like mere glimpses into single moments of the creators' lives. They all collate into this anthology, which is designed as an exhibition in printed form. The works are presented for readers to browse at their leisure, focus as intently as desired, or be guided from start to finish as curated to balance the peaks in emotions and pace of the individual styles.

*Oh, How We Laughed** is the second book in the Blue Feet Anthology series and is edited by Alex Dunkin. The first book in the series, *Green*, is an anthology by South Australian emerging creative researchers.

Cover artwork: queer snuggles and giggles

This cover was made by queer, trans, Aboriginal (Narrunga, Kaurna, Ngarrindjeri) artist Tikari Rigney.

'I feel very proud to have made this cover to hug the stories of beautiful, talented queer, disabled artists on Kaurna Yarta. I hope this artwork with its cosy imagery and colours holds you as you step into our little world.'—Tikari Rigney.

Copyright © 2024

Oh, How We Laughed*: A Blue Feet Anthology as a collective work is copyright of anthology editor Dr Alex Dunkin and Buon-Cattivi Press. Individual contributions remain the sole copyright of the contributing creatives as named in this anthology.

All rights reserved.

ISBN (paperback): 978-1-922314-13-0
ISBN (ebook): 978-1-922314-14-7

This is a creative and artistic work. Names, characters, places, and incidents either are the product of the author's imagination or are used creatively for the purpose of artistic expression. Any further resemblance to actual events, locales, organisations, or persons, living or dead, is entirely coincidental and beyond the intent of the creator.

Buon-Cattivi Press operates on the land of the Kaurna people. We pay our respects to elders past and present. We acknowledge that sovereignty was never ceded, and recognise and respect their ongoing cultural heritage, beliefs, and relationship with the land.

Additional editing by Cameron Rutherford
Cover art by Tikari Rigney.
Typesetting by Andrew Crooks.

Oh, How We Laughed*

A Blue Feet Anthology

Buon-Cattivi Press
Kaurna Country
Adelaide, Australia

Proceeds from sales of this book are distributed to CRIPS, Pay The Rent, and the creators published within *Oh, How We Laughed*.

Contents

Editor's Notes	12
Curators' Notes	14

Tabitha Lean | Budhin Mingaan
    Ssshhhh!   19

Denver Rurrk
    Portraits   29

J.A.M.
    November 2023//Blood-gazing   37

Tikari Rigney
    Kamami, ngarrpadla, ngangkita and enby   49
    The expired use by date of a crusty old white woman   57
    Country Remembers you   59

Rainier Hotchkiss
    Snail Does Recovery   61

Tushar Patel
    Brrr: The Hope in Winter   67

Jace Reh
    Blak, Broke, Crazy and Trans   83

KJ Hepworth
    Legacy   91

Sally Ann Hunter
    Hurt   101

Victoria Knight
    attn: the ivory tower   109

Fig Kershaw
    Messy Minds Are Magical   117

Cameron Rutherford
    Summer Cut   127
    Send   135
    The Extinction of Boys   139

Theo Brown
    sketches of the bodymind   151

Leon McAloney
    The Truest Letter I Ever Wrote   163

Freddie Foeng
    Pages of a Lifetime   180

Editor's Notes
by Dr Alex Dunkin

I was first approached by co-curator of *Oh, How We Laughed** Jace through a colleague, Dante, to consider this anthology after Jace connected with the first Blue Feet Anthology, *Green*. That project was an experimental work with a group of emerging South Australian creative researchers, including Dante. Witnessing the varying approaches to writing and storytelling was a stimulating and inspiring experience for me. I knew after completing *Green* I wanted to expand the series and had some ideas floating around. I felt a strong connection to the concept of *Oh How We Laughed** from the moment I heard Jace's pitch and knew I wanted this to be the next book in the anthology series.

The experience of 'always feeling different growing up' resonated with me deeply. A queer neurodivergent child growing up in rural South Australia, I had all the makings for being the odd one out. It took me until my twenties to realise it wasn't the common experience to be able to, on a whim, do things like vividly recall memories, facts, and—what I would later learn are social scripts—behaviours from decades prior, to navigate memories as if following a map dotted with signposts. In fact, it was often a struggle for me to escape these memories and to break away from seemingly established social rules. It amazed me how others were able to just let things go, diverge from patterns, and move on. There's bluntness to my memories, events appearing in my head just as they were experienced in the moment, without the embellishment and adornments that help people cope. The trope of comedy equals tragedy plus time was foreign to me; I couldn't natural diminish memories. After surviving sexual assault in my late 20s, my memory function become a liability to my mental health, and it was through seeking treatment for the subsequent PTSD that I was lead down the path that ultimately provided an autism diagnosis in adulthood.

Since then, I've nested in myself as a proudly queer, autistic, admin gay and settled in the many different hats and masks I wear in life. I'm incredibly proud of my work running Buon-Cattivi Press. I find a lot of joy in having a micro-publishing label. There's room to play and experiment with a wide range of writers without the pressures of a full commercial process. The boutique nature of the label grants time and space with each project. It also provides time for me to learn about authors and their own approaches in presenting their voices. Part of this learning is recognising that I'm in a privileged position where I have the ability to platform more marginalised voices. It is also such an honour that writers, artists, and creators to entrust me with their work and voices. When compiling submissions into the final manuscript for this anthology, the biggest considerations came back to maintaining space and time. I didn't want to risk a haphazard placement with a crammed narrative style to the anthology order. I hope you enjoy sitting with each of these incredible creators and experiencing the layers of their creative styles.

Oh, How We Laughed* is intentionally asterisked. 'Laughed' can be replaced by many words that no doubt will appear to you after reading these stories. There is laughter but also pain, hope, discovery, grief, and many other emotions that come and go, or, in some cases, outstay their welcome. The words and images might come from whispers, riotous laughter, or even just subtle body language. The key point is the voices are there and I believe it's a duty of those who have the ability to amplify those voices. No matter the size of the platform, we should share the art and the stories of our communities to the overall chorus.

Curators' Notes
by Jace Reh

Acknowledgement of Country

This book has been edited and published on the stolen lands of the Kaurna people. Submissions for this book have been written on the lands of the Kaurna, Ngarrindjeri, Narrunga and Boandik people, and we extend our respect and adoration to the ancestors, elders and powerful communities of these lands.

I stand on the shoulders of giants, the Gamilaroi people, and am grateful for the opportunity to work beside my communities to bring this work and hold a mirror to this oppressive system. We cannot have disability justice or queer liberation without first called for Blak sovereignty and Land Back. Under the colonial regime of so-called Australia, stories and culture have been attacked and destroyed by settlers, and we wish to platform these stories to take back this control.

Introducing Theo and Jace

Our love story started the way any two gay disabled trans men could in the middle of a pandemic: on Grindr. I moved to Adelaide a week earlier and spotted his cute curls in the sea of faceless torsos. I have no idea how he fell into my distance range, living on the other side of metropolitan Adelaide, but I was happy he did. We were both quite reserved, met once, and I really didn't know if it would go any further. But it did, and as I write this, we are creeping towards our fourth year together. We've seen a lot in this time, the slashing of the NDIS, a new parliament in so-called Australia, the election of Sinn Fein in Northern Ireland, an ever-rising death toll in Palestine… but more than that we've seen things together. Three paid presentations discussing our own experiences and sharing the learnings of Disability Justice, forming a Disability collective and standing on parliament steps calling for an end to Aboriginal deaths in custody. That was not where we expected to see our Grindr hookup go.

It took a while to share secrets between us, as any relationship does. Something many people in this book will know about, telling an intimate partner, or anyone really, that you're disabled isn't an easy task. You don't know how they will react. You don't know if this is the thing that makes you become 'too much'. I need to sleep for close to ten hours a night to feed the monster that is my fatigue, and Theo is lucky to get more than five hours with the beast of insomnia. Bit of an odd pairing, I can assure you. But we make it work. One of the funniest pairings we have, is one that really brought us together to make this anthology a reality. I am quite dyslexic, but I love books. Theo is incredibly anxious about the sound of his own voice, but loves reading. So, when a book comes out, like the inspiration for this one, *Nothing to Hide: Voices of Trans and Gender-Diverse Australia*, I would never get to truly enjoy it.

That was until Theo offered to sit with me on the couch and read out loud for hours on end, so I could enjoy every moment, without having to take forty minutes to read a single page. *Care Work: Dreaming Disability Justice* was read to me in this fashion. Leah Lakshmi is such an icon, sharing their beautiful, raw self, an inspiration we shared in a way accessible to our disabled body-minds. When Theo spent two years in and out of specialist consulting rooms desperate for a diagnosis to understand why he was at war with his body, I was there with my unavoidable obnoxious questions demanding he be listened to when it became too draining for him to do the demanding himself. When I needed to share my story, as a blackfulla effected by the prison industrial complex for generations, Theo sat down and typed every word while I dictated it to him.

These acts may seem small to a neurotypical, able-bodied, white, cishet person, but for us, they were the reason we could achieve the life we wanted, desired, and deserved. There were moments of tears, and pain, but moments, like the title, where, oh, how we laughed. I think often of Lou Sullivan, whose diaries are titled 'We Both Laughed In Pleasure', and feel my heart warm. A chronically ill trans man, who could think only of the moments of laughter.

We have shared laughs with this anthology's contributors, and tears, and smiles, and belted out singalongs. We share our stories with one another, and now as the reader, we share them with you. These stories come from across South Australia, spanning Kaurna, Ngarrindjeri, Narrunga and Boandik country, including Aboriginal, Pakistani, Tamil and Asian voices. All works are created by Queer and Disabled folks, and primarily gender-diverse folks too! These voices are often forgotten. None of this would be possible without the always kind Alex Dunkin of Buon-Cattivi Press, who managed to fight my pathological demand avoidance and helped me put pen to paper, or in this case, fingers to keyboard.

Oh, How We Laughed*

A Blue Feet Anthology

Ssshhhh!

by Tabitha Lean | Budhin Mingaan

Creator Bio

Her name is Tabitha, or as her ancestors know her, Budhin Mingaan. She is a First Nations woman living, loving, creating and dreaming on Kaurna Yerta. She is a published poet, writer, spoken word and visual artist, exploring the tension between the new and old worlds, and the spaces in between. She believes that who we are and what we are comes from the alchemy of our struggles, and all of her work, from her poetry to her pyrography and weaving seeks to honour the old, while traversing the present to carve out a future that holds within it both possibility and promise. She's also an abolition activist determined to disrupt the colonial project and abolish the prison industrial complex—and she's fucking angry, channelling every bit of that rage towards challenging the colonial carceral state.

Artist Statement

I am a criminalised woman living with a significant mental illness. I know the power of stories like mine being heard because voices like mine have largely been marginalised. My presence, and indeed my voice, challenges the hegemony the colony continues to hold over 'legitimate' knowledge about the Aboriginal existence and counters the incessant reproduction of racialised dynamics and white stories favoured and valorised by the literati. My work seeks to disrupt these canons, and challenges people to think differently about what people can teach us about state violence by changing the way we see stories being told, and by whom.

Ssshhhh!

I've got a secret.

Actually, I've got a whole bunch of secrets.

A whole pocket full of 'em tucked away. Tucked away so tightly that they rest beneath my rib cage threatening to burst out of my chest at any moment. In fact, I feel like the only reason they stay within me is that I've gaffer-taped the little box that they are stored in and shoved it so far back in my chest cavity that every time they shuffle forward and try to bulge out of my body to see the light of day, I've got enough warning that I can bully them back into submission.

But if you think about it, secrets are a funny thing.

The secrets we keep. The secrets we tell. The secrets we hold. The secrets we share. The secrets that fester. The dirty little secrets that brew into even uglier canker sores. The funny little secrets shared between lovers. The secret glances. The secret deals.

...the secrets that rest behind walls of silence.

leans forward, purses lips, nods head

Those...those are the secrets I know best.

lean back, grins

Ah fuck! Let's face it, I know all the secrets.
I know the kinds of secrets that get me in trouble.

winks eye, taps side of nose with pointer finger

I know other people's secrets. I know the secrets of violent and lecherous men. I know the secrets of angry fathers. I know the secrets of flirty boys with wandering hands. I know the secrets of those who took more than they were entitled to. I know the secrets of those who did forbidden things to forbidden people in forbidden ways in forbidden places.

I hold so many secrets for so many people, and absolutely none of them are mine to keep. My hands are so full of other people's secrets they threaten to seep through my fingers like running water. My brain is a catalogue of other people's shame. I wear their dishonour like a winter coat, and that fucker is so heavy my shoulders droop beneath the weight of it.

But lately I've been thinking it's time for a new coat. The season's changed and winter's long gone. Summer's here and I'm hot and bothered. It's getting humid and I'm beginning to sweat. But no matter how hard I try to get rid of the fucking ghosts, I just can't shake off the shackles of other people's secrets. They hang around my neck like a noose. The secrets I keep only serve to protect others. If I spill any of them, the horse will bolt and I'll be left swinging from the tree, legs flailing as my throat gets squeezed and every last bit of oxygen leaves my body.

Shoot the messenger.

points fingers into the shape of a gun, clicks tongue

Bang!. You're dead.

So where does this leave me? A woman skidding towards fifty at lightning speed, body loaded up with backpacks full of other people's secrets weighing me down, dragging on me so I walk like my feet are in quicksand?

All I want to do is go back to this one magical moment.

pinches finger and thumb together

This one tiny moment in time.

I don't even remember it. I only know it from a photograph. A little square faded polaroid, one I rescued from a pile at my dad's house. I carry it with me everywhere as if its sheer proximity to my body could magic up its existence. As if a portal could open up and transport me.

The photograph was taken in 1976. You know how I know? Because it's got my mum and me in it. She was killed by the time I was one, so it's got to be then.

leans forward, photo in hand

In the photo, I'm wearing a loose nappy, a baggy t-shirt, a dummy pinned to my top and my mouth is opened wide in a silent laugh. My mother (her name's Glenys for those of you who never met her) is holding one of my hands to steady my chubby little legs as I try to stumble-run with tentative baby steps. Her face. Oh, it's her face.

furrows brow

Her face is the face of adoration and love and happiness and devotion and kindness and love and love and love and love and love. Did I mention love? Did I? Did I? Because she radiates love. Like actual love. Fucking sunrays and moonbeams and rainbow unicorn tear drops of love for me. All of it for me. Just at the sight of me. She radiates a kind of love I have never seen, let alone known... other than from a tiny little polaroid.

And you know what? That love wasn't tucked into a tiny pocket in the back of her faded flared jeans. That love wasn't a dirty little secret. That love wasn't conditional on my compliance, my body, my behaviour, my weight, my silence, my work output, my finances, my potential, my grades, my anything. It was for me. Just for me.

stillness
silence

This was a time before worry furrowed my brow and carved lines across my forehead. A time before crinkles formed at the edges of my eyes. A time before the scars of deceit and anger lay across my body like great fault lines. A time before I was worn down and abused. A time before I knew how and when to cower and hide. A time before I knew when to be silent when to shout, when to speak up, and when to retreat, when to flinch and when to hit back.

A time before I was burdened by other people.

A lighter time.

My time.

A time when my body was mine.

A time when my mind was mine.

A time when my heart was mine.

A time when someone looked at me with love and hope and care and promise.

A time when my backpack was full of clean clothes and balm and warm milk—not lies, empty promises, unfulfilled dreams, and filthy little secrets.

Fucking hell.

Secrets?

shakes head

Who the fuck would have them…?

leans back, folds arm, bows head
nothingness
silence

....

......

...

..

.

Portraits

by Denver Rurrk

Creator Bio

Denver Rurrk finds it hard to call themself an artist, like many queers who suffer from imposter syndrome, but especially since their various work doesn't bring in money currently, is frequently digital, and often involves tracing. However, they continue to remind themself that these things do not make their art any less valid. Their art usually features animals, nature, and queer themes, showing a love for both the natural world and the knowledge that being queer is natural too. Through their work, they want to help normalise and push for more diverse representation, in all its forms and intersections, in popular media. By incorporating queerness in their art, Denver hopes to help create a world where everyone's differences are celebrated and normalised, so being "strange", "weird" or "different" loses any negative connotations and is a state desired by all. With some pieces they want you to just enjoy their abstract nature and know that it makes you gay simply by experiencing it (as per THE agenda).

Artist Statements

Self-Portrait

This half nude self-portrait was an artistic attempt to develop greater appreciation of one's own skin. This process helped lead me to eventually realise my deep desire for gender-affirming top-surgery. I'm depicted with my beloved cat, Couscous, who, despite being a demon at times, remains a favourite child. Inspired by Laura Callaghan's approach of portraying people without smiling or being 'camera ready', this piece offers a realistic glimpse into a moment of the daily life of a queer individual. The portrayal aims to provide an authentic insight into queer life at home, and a rare moment when the artist isn't putting a smile on for themself or others.

Medieval Family Portrait

Inspired by medieval cat paintings, often humorously inaccurate as if created by artists who had never seen cats, this queer family portrait integrates the often-overlooked presence of LGBTQ+ individuals in historical contexts. Seeking medieval depictions of queer figures, the search term 'gay medieval portrait' led to a painting called 'The Sodom of the North', which forms the backdrop for this queer grouping. Everyone in the portrait, including the fur bébés, use they/them pronouns, and each bring unique personalities to the composition. This piece aims to reclaim history, challenge traditional norms, and celebrate the diverse forms of families throughout time.

November 2023//
Blood-gazing

by J.A.M.

Creator Bio

J.A.M. (ze/hir, they/them) is a multi-disciplinary creative, who was born in Rawalpindi, Pakistan, and has resided on Kaurna land for most of hir life. Ze is a student of digital media and engineering, a writer, an amateur actor, and a musician, as well as a visual artist who operates in a variety of mediums. J.A.M. is interested in exploring a broad range of themes, from power dynamics and socio-political issues to the power of friendship and how to stay silly in unsilly times. You can see hir work on instagram @jam.exe7 or on tumblr @jam-exe.

Artist Statement

November 2023//Blood-gazing is a piece deeply tied to my own experiences with the idea that all struggles are interconnected. This piece, and a lot of my work, comes from the belief that it takes vulnerability to confront the ways in which systems have marginalised and will continue to marginalise you, and others around the world. It comes from the belief that taking the courage to look at these issues directly, and to confront them head on, allows for the creation of tools to empowerment, and thus is key to dismantling those very systems.

Truth is a complicated, subjective, and multi-faceted thing, which makes it extremely large and challenging to hold. The path to truth is full of uncertainty too, and people tend to shy away from uncertainty. But there is no justice without truth. However complicated, painful, challenging, or confusing the pieces may be, this work hopes to speak to a facet of the truth I hold.

November 2023//Blood-gazing

In November of 2023, I made friends on the steps of parliament. He was a young Palestinian man, and we were at a rally for the lives of his people, his family. We sat together, waiting for the march to get back from Hindmarsh Square.

He didn't have to wait with me. My wheelchair had broken down that morning, and it was my first day walking, one week after nose surgery. I couldn't follow my friends down the chanting route with the other strong hundreds. He didn't seem to have any such reason to stay.

It was hot and hazy, that late spring Sunday, and the air was charged with electrified grief made into action.

The speeches had ended, but I could still hear the woman reading the Rafeef Ziadah poem:

> *Today, my body was a TV'd massacre that had to fit into soundbites and word limits.*

I could still see how the maple leaves from the tall city trees had paused mid-air and hung to listen.

I needed to do something, so I promised an older man I'd look after the organisers' boxes as he got the car. That's when the young man—a boy who appeared to be slightly younger than me, yet carried himself as much older—came and sat down beside me.

He asked why I came in such a serious tone, and I spluttered a moment. My mind was baked in the sun, and my nose was still dripping blood under my mask.

I paused before saying, 'Because it's right.' and then, I tried to crack the awkwardness by saying, 'I'm not a big fan of genocide.'

That broke the tension, and he felt less like an old man on a mission. We began to joke, like youths do, back and forth about horrific things. Then he thanked me for being there, and I felt queasy again.

In between our exchanges were pauses, and I watched his family mill back and forth. They spoke in Arabic to each other, as they organised and gathered up the remaining protest supplies. I saw some girls, presumably his younger sisters, only teenagers, helping too. They reminded me so much of my own big messy gatherings back home, in Pakistan. A painful nostalgia.

My new friend spoke proudly of his father, who was on the council of the activist group. I asked how long he'd personally been in it, and he said a few years. He explained how it helped with survivors' guilt—his family were lucky to be rich and educated, to get out alive and safe. I looked up at the sun while he spoke. It felt easier than making eye contact.

I can't help but feel my words came out poorly. He was gracious, though. Too gracious. I told him how it wasn't the same, but my family had moved to avoid war too. We were lucky in that same way, but we also caused some of the problems we left behind.

I don't know what compelled me to tell a stranger, but on a day where thousands gathered to beg people to listen, it felt dishonest not to say it.

I told him about my grandfather, who had acted as a right hand of a dictator named Zia Ul Haq. Of my grandfather's brother, who had been part of the ISI, the spy service that helped the CIA create the Taliban. How it all created the situation in Pakistan today, where Afghan refugees were being ethnically cleansed as we spoke.

He told me he had heard about the mass deportation too, and asked if I knew any way to help. My floundering returned, realising and explaining, that as much as I had spread the information I had found out about the horror, I still didn't know what anyone could do from overseas. I resolved to find out more, as much as I could. I had to do better.

My new friend told me, reassured me that I wasn't my ancestors, of course. Everyone tells me this, and I tried to believe him. I try to believe them.

However, on this charged, dream-like afternoon, I had just been out of surgery, and I had been feeling far too much since then—something to do with having my face cut open, then stitched back together, perhaps.

Or maybe something to do with recovering at my mother's house, which always seemed to tear something out of me, deeper than tissue.

Just before surgery, I had taken some notes. I had written:

> *I'm in the hospital, pre op in bed with my glasses off. Everything is a soft hazy hospital blue.*
> *I feel like a child with my too big gown and too skinny body drowning in the washed-out lights.*
> *The nurse was lovely, and she's a person, so are the doctors, and other nurses, so of course I'm not alone.*
> *...*
> *And I kind of wish I wasn't alone right now.*
> *It's not that I'm afraid, I'm just tired and sad of going through so many life events with just myself by my own side.*
> *...*
> *I guess I'll play an audiobook.*
> *I don't have my glasses on, they're in a tub with my name labelled, on the bedside table.*
> *Besides it will be nice to have a voice by me for just a little while longer.*

The week after the surgery I spent at my mother's house. I kept seeing my own teenaged dead body decaying into various points of that structure. I was avoiding mirrors, washing my hands over and over, trying to be clean, the same way I used to as a child. My dead high school friend would visit at night, playing one last joke in my dreams—pretending she never died.

This isn't a metaphor. I was having hallucinations. No, they felt more like visions. No, more like the breaking of the veil of time. I could see every lonely version of myself, at every age in that house, carrying out their sentence, separated and layered over one another.

Maybe there was something about seeing my own blood, tasting it mixed with the salt of the cleaning solution and my tears, that helped create the off-balance feeling. Or maybe it was just those end months, the embers of the year, and how they always burn me into hazy smoke.

Every so often, my new friend would get up from our place at the parliament steps, walk across the path, take a sip of water from a bottle, and spit behind a tree. I thought nothing of it the first time, but by the second time, I was watching him, concerned. I became even more concerned when I noticed his spit was red. When he came back, I asked if he was ok.

He told me, somewhat self-consciously, that he had mouth issues. This is when I revealed that I had recently had surgery, and that I still had a large bloody bandage on under my mask. I think we understood each other's shaky grace a bit better after that exchange.

Some cops tried to hurry us along, but we waved them off.

As his family finished packing up, he opted to stay and keep talking, which surprised me even further. We exchanged pieces of our lives: our degrees and Instagrams and dreams—much more average conversation. Still, we kept coming back to liberation, and how there was no silver lining to genocide—but God at least there were people here, witnessing now. At least that.

Grief and hope and grief and hope.

He bid me goodbye as marchers started to trickle back down the street. I met back up with my friends, and we were swallowed up by the body of the crowd.

A week later, after the march, I was trying to stay true to my private promise. I was looking into ways I could help Afghans in Pakistan. Fortunately, there was activism in Pakistan fighting the government for the rights of refugees. Less fortunately, there didn't appear to be much to do in solidarity from overseas, not that anyone had planned so far.

Then I fell, with a sinking feeling in my stomach, into a rabbit hole of research, as I discovered some details about a massacre known as Black September. And as I dove deeper, I saw history layer again, as some familiar names began to pop up.

I can't untangle the threads of history neatly, or unbiasedly, or even very cleverly. Still, I'll try to explain as best as I can what I learned, as I scanned through news articles, Wikipedia, and the only academic text I could access, which was written by an ex-CIA agent.

In 1950, Jordan annexed the West Bank of Gaza, and what followed was decades of unrest. By the early 1970s, the Jordanian army, along with all the big players of the region—the CIA, Henry Kissinger, Israel, and neighbouring Arab states—had come together to wage war on the guerrilla liberation fighters of the annexed Palestinian refugee camps.

This war, Black September, would begin in September of 1970, and end in July 1971. This is where my own unfortunate star of the story comes in—a then little-known military commander from Pakistan, a man named Zia Ul Haq. This man, who my grandfather went to military school with, helped to command and deploy Jordan's army. This exercise would lead, in total, to the deaths of around 3,500 Palestinians. This is how Ul Huq would make his name, and place him in the position to one day become the dictator my grandfather served.

Later that day, my mother, who was born in April of 1971, called me for her occasional check in.

I asked her about Ul Haq and the war and grandfather, and she said, 'Stop looking up things. It was a long time ago'.

Maybe I'd been staring into my own blood in the bathroom sink too much those past few weeks. Still, it strikes me that I was benefiting from a life away from bombs, and a recovery with clean running water—even if it wasn't hot water thanks to my landlord. How could I not be culpable?

Maybe I'm talking too much about myself again. Trapping myself in cycles. I'll wash this blood clot down the sink and end this story.

Stories like this are a dime a dozen. I know being connected to this one doesn't change that it happened. That people have been hurt.

History weaves its web through all of us. Everyone I have marched with over these months, we have marched on occupied land too. Many of us, most of us, have been intertwined with, culpable in those stories too.

My nose has ceased spitting up flesh now. I'm breathing easier than I ever have before. Wounds contain the signs of the body healing, being rebuilt better. So maybe it would do us all some good to see our own blood more often.

Kamami, ngarrpadla, ngangkita and enby

~

The expired use by date of a crusty old white woman

~

Country Remembers you

by Tikari Rigney

Creator Bio

Tikari Rigney is a non-binary Kaurna, Narrunga and Ngarrindjeri visual artist and poet. Their practice references their queer bodily experience, Aboriginality, and the complexities of being a silly boi. They explore themes of humour, rebirth, and emotional vulnerability.

Artist Statement

I write so I can figure out how the hell to live. I hope these little writings help others live in this delightful, tricky space we call our homes, our bodies, our minds, our Country.

Kamami, ngarrpadla, ngangkita and enby
Written on Kaurna Country

Nana, aunty, mother and enby

Powerful
Nurturer
Feminine warriors

Leaders
Movers and shakers
From a strong line of powerful Aboriginal women

24 the age of saying but a life of knowing,
Connect and disconnect to my feminine.

The in-between

Body dysphoria, yet powerful history
A genderless body, yet honouring my ancestors
Women's business, is it mine any longer?

Once a woman, now no longer
A history imbedded in my bones and curvaceous flesh
Passed from generations of kamami, ngarrpadla, ngangkita to enby

I can see my nana in my hands
See my aunties in my pupils
And feel my mum in my heart

Their spirit is in me and mine in them.

The expired use by date of a crusty old white woman
Written on Kaurna Country

Oh the Queen
Oh the so called mourning and insurmountable loss

Needing to take a day, aye?

Public holiday willy nilly just cos

Newspaper, insta, internet unsafe

Queen, Queen, Queen,
Colony, Colony, Colony

The expired use by date of a crusty old white woman, the figurehead of Aboriginal murder and stolen land

Is this really more important than
First nations suffering?
Stolen land?
Intergenerational trauma?

Vomit react

In life and death you are not my matriarch
and you never will be.

Country Remembers you
Written on Peramangk Country

Wind feathers the grass,

As it blows my heart away from you and towards me

Listen, listen, papa says,
Listen as the ancestors whisper in the wind

What does Gurratah say?
Can you hear Nori's call back to Country?
Narrunga, Ngarrindjeri seas
Whispering,
Calling me back for a reset.

Sneak peek into the future,
Connection to the past,
Anchoring in the present

Lay down my body
Becomes the cliffs rippled with history,
My hair,
The rush lapped up by the banks of the Coorong
My change forever recognised
Welcome back home,
Back to Country.

Snail Does Recovery

by Rainier Hotchkiss

Creator Bio

Creating on Kaurna Country, Rainier Hotchkiss (they/them) is a passionate zine-maker, illustrator, painter and resource-creator. Their work merges their Autistic special interests (snails!) with their experience of mental illness, psych wards, loss, disability and queerness. They can be found @rainyday_friends on Instagram.

Artist Statement

The initial draft of Snail Does Recovery was created in the midst of a self-harm relapse crisis. It helped me find my way back to myself.

Snails became a special interest of mine just after my first psych ward stay. This was a traumatic time of loud emotions, panicked suicidal thoughts, and fast-paced chaotic change. Coming across snails on the sidewalk and stopping to watch for as long as I needed brought me rare relief, solace, and joy.

My dear friend Eloise understood this, and her unconditional love of me and my snail companions saved my life. I met Eloise in the psych ward and she was the strongest, funniest and most compassionate person I have ever known. She died in 2022 and hoped I would stay despite my intense grief and learn to love myself.

Since then, I have continued to love and often see myself in snails—their slow persistence, need for quiet and gentleness and ability to heal in supportive environments. Even feeling unwanted by a majority, moving my body in ways others judge, or using coping strategies that no longer work or fit the circumstances. I learnt to love myself through them.

Snail does recovery

getting better takes slow progress — but look how far you've come

---

sometimes it's hard to see — it seems like I haven't come very far *...when I've actually come sooo far from start*

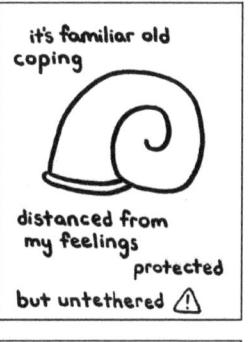

even if I know things have got better from worse before — it feels awful — so I retreat

it's familiar old coping — distanced from my feelings, protected but untethered ⚠

---

the feelings always kick back — ouch — more intense than before

I remember they just want listened to for example:

Sad	tells you what you value & that you need comfort
fear	you need to be careful + to feel safe
anger	you need to make change + problem solve
lonely	you need connection

I ground myself — see I'm not alone

---

bring on the storm (it's still hard)

feeling my feelings I am so **alive** — connected, strong, real, myself, full of love — it's always worth it

made on Kaurna land

for the hurting, hiding, dissociating, suicidal, self harming, recovering, relapsing, trying-again and feeling everything

for Eloise who loved me + my snails ;

Brrr: The Hope in Winter

by Tushar Patel

Creator Bio

Tushar K. Patel, is an Indigenous/Tribal artist from India who practices in various mediums such as words, colours, flora (dead or alive), clay, papier-mâché, henna, paintings and rangoli.

Artist Statement

This work is focused on people struggling with mental health and life, how simple things become challenged and overcome, or hurdles to be dealt with.

Text:

Brrr: The Hope in Winter
Odd wind on my path,
Cold, dark and gloom!
I wonder where to go
Walk in silence in the dark,
Can't see any footprints!
Brrr!
I don't know when she came
out and inside me myself!
I shall wait for thee to come,
bright, jolly and pleasant!

-Tushar Patel

Brrr - The Hope in winter

Odd wind on my path,
cold, dark and gloomy!
I wonder where to go?
it's slow, dusky and foggy!
Walk in silence in a dark,
Can't see any footprit aside!
Brrr!
I don't know when she came?,
out and inside me myself!
I shall wait for thee to come,
bright, jolly and pleasant!

— Tushar Patel

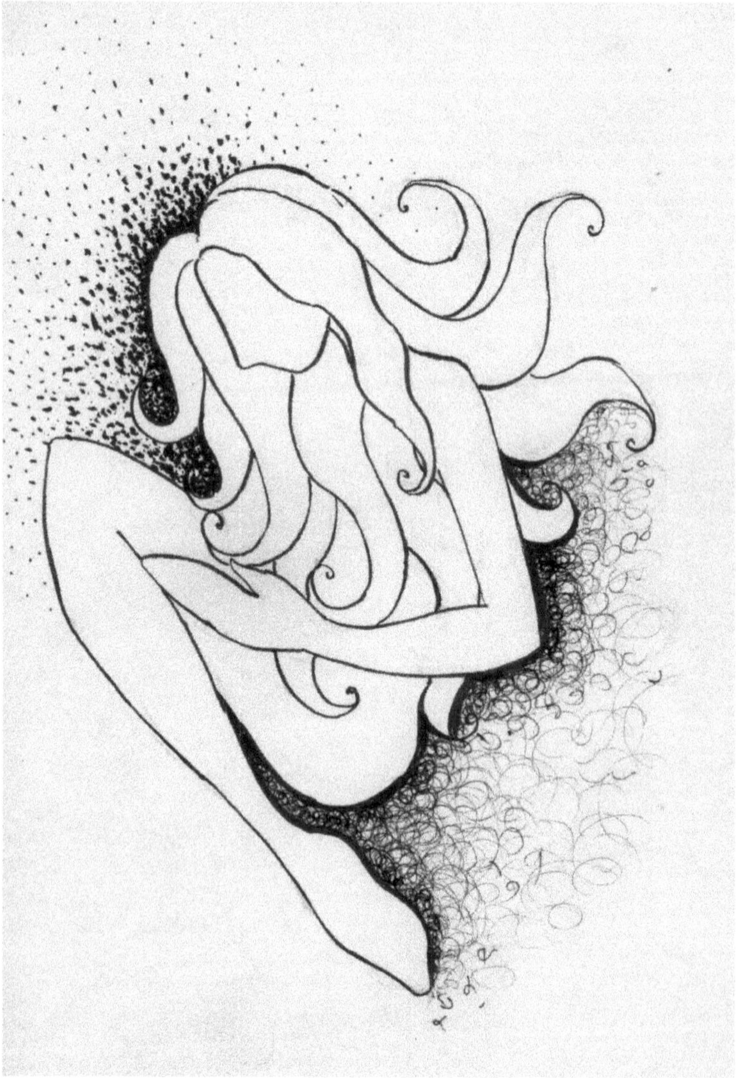

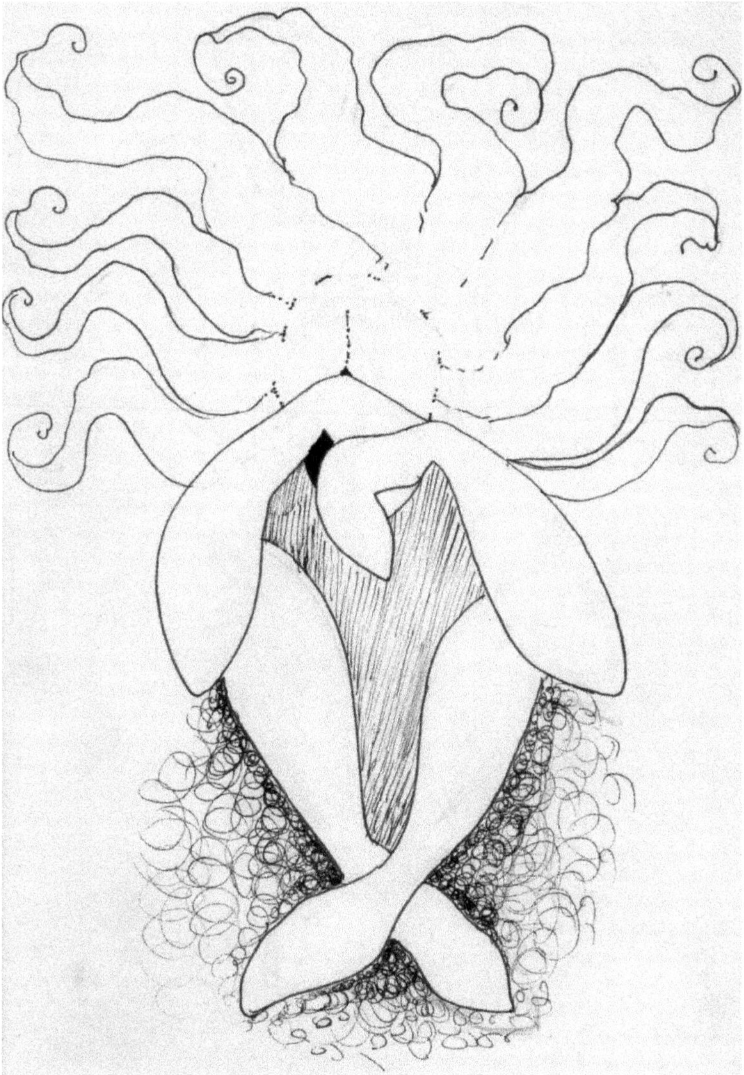

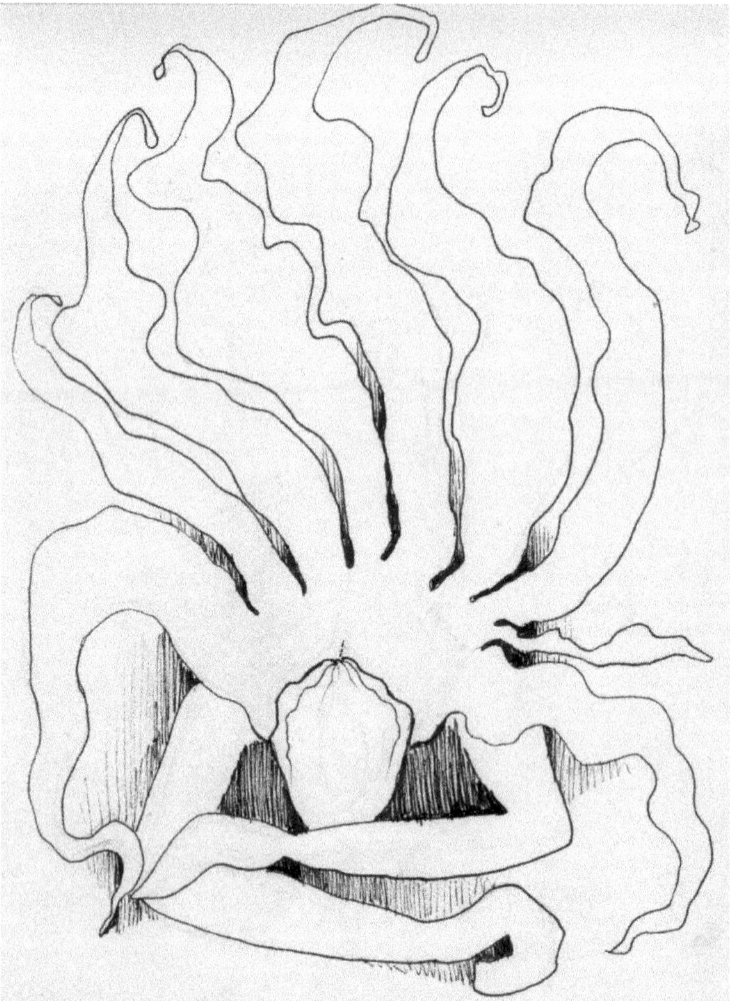

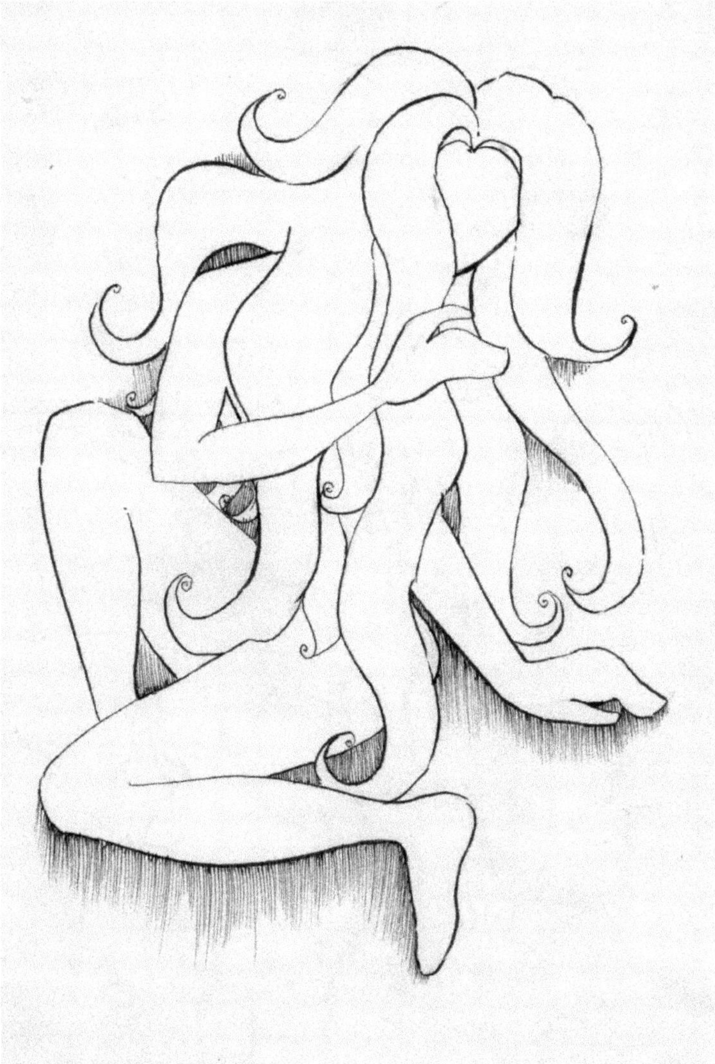

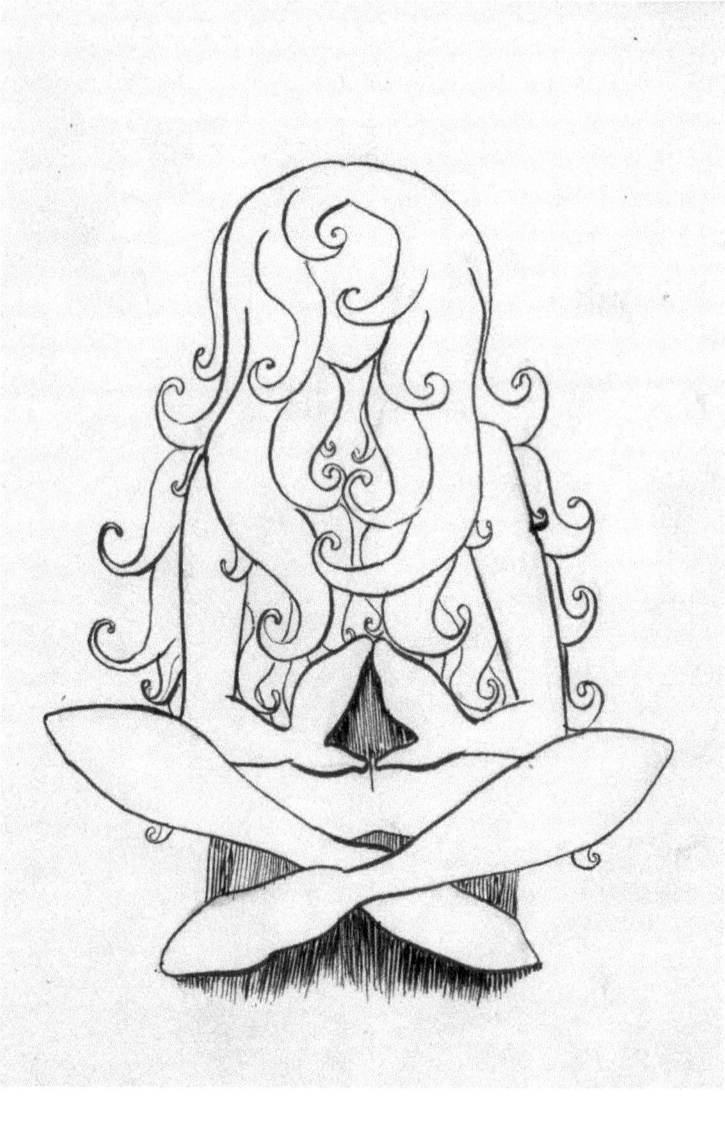

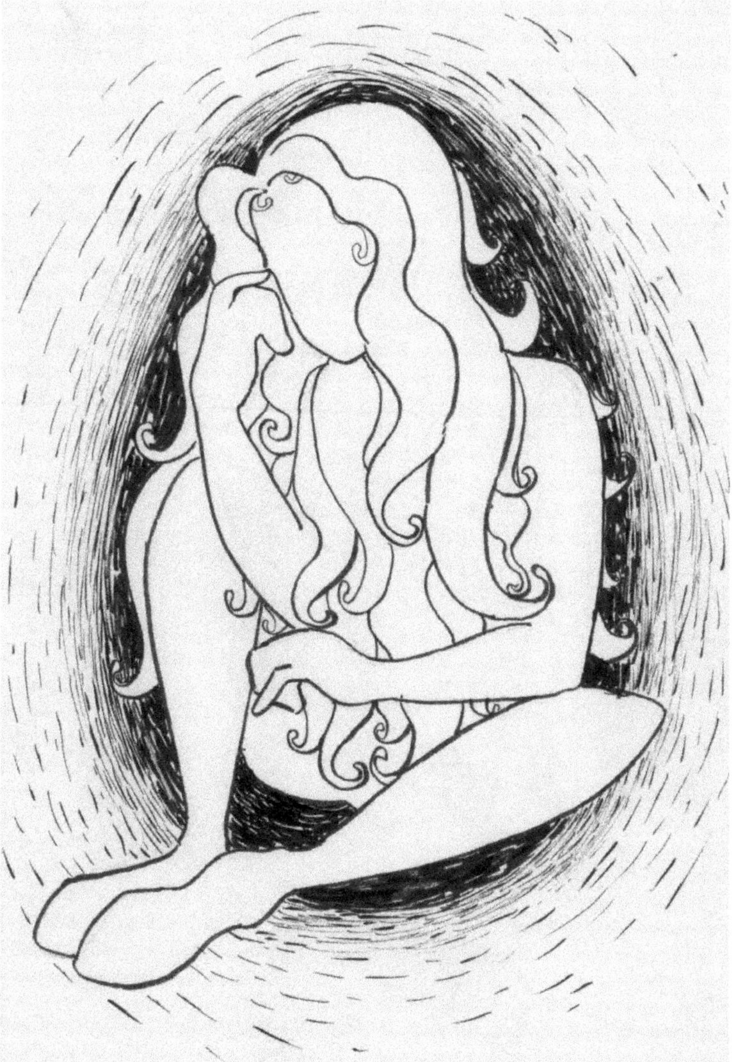

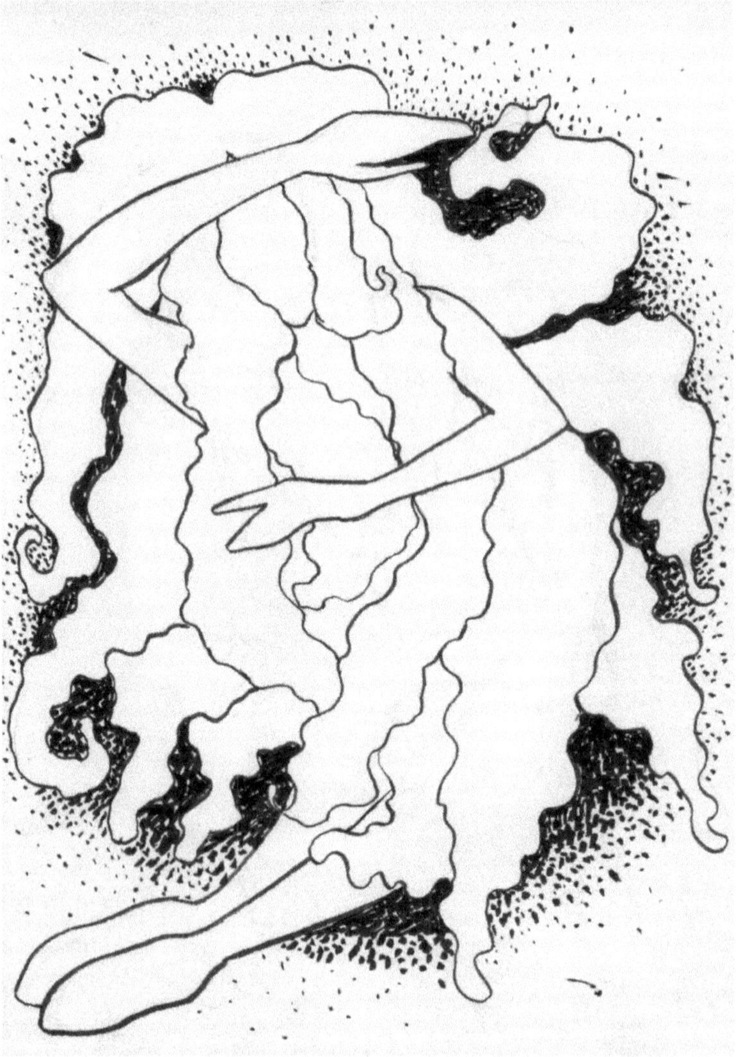

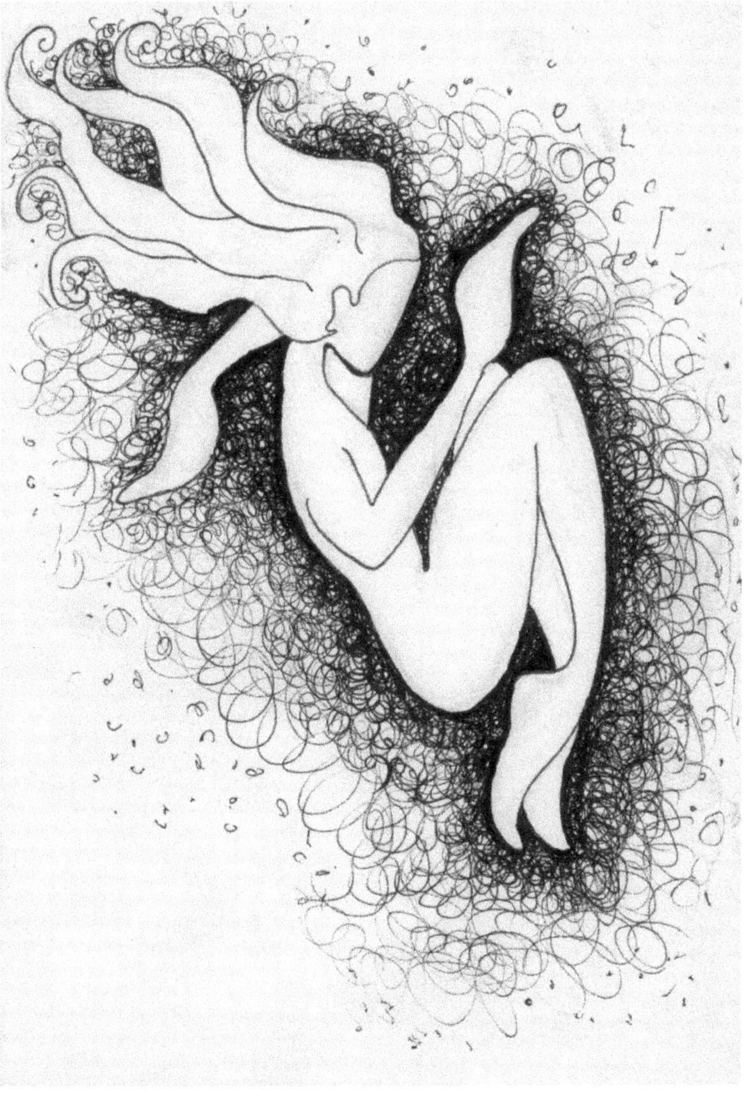

Blak, Broke, Crazy and Trans

by Jace Reh

Creator Bio

Jace Reh (he/she/they) is a queer, disabled Gamilaroi person living on Kaurna Yerta, raised on Narrunga country. With a passion for words and social justice, she endeavours to create deeply personal works that speak to his journeys of self-discovery and community building. Jace and their partner Theo have created Collaborative Radical Intersectional Performance Spaces (CRIPS) in the hopes of bringing together non-normative body-minds to create the perfect space to learn from one another.

Artist Statement

My piece 'Blak, Broke, Crazy and Trans' uses the rule of three to keep these four words stuck in the reader's mind. We often will take one moment or one interaction with a person to define them. This piece tells my story through that lens, seeing at which point I meet the expectations of a stereotype, followed by 'that's pretty [Blak/broke/crazy/trans]'. These four terms, irrespective of their weaponisation throughout my life, are integral to the way in which I see myself and others are capable of seeing me.

Blak, Broke, Crazy and Trans

I knew I was **Blak** from when I was young.
My mum knew very little of her people,
So I sat down in front of the TV and watched their animated dream times.
All my best friends at school were **Blak**.
It was just easier to exist with them than with anyone else.
We just *got* each other in ways no one else could.
My great grandfather died a year to the day before I was born.
My mum swore he visited her in a dream and said he would pass his spirit to me.
Now that's pretty **Blak**.

I knew we were **broke** pretty young too.
When I was born my dad worked long hours driving trucks,
And all my clothes were second hand,
Unless wealthier family members bought gifts.
We lived in a **broke** part of town,
Housing commissions and recently released homes.
I remember my Auntie invited us to dinner for her 40th
And me, Dad and my baby sister shared one meal,
From Hogs Breath Café.
Now that's pretty **broke**.

It took me a little longer to realise I was **crazy**.
I first tried to kill myself when I was 6.
I thought if I could pull my bookshelf down on to me maybe I would die.
It sounds **crazy** now but I just knew I needed to die.
I got hospitalised for the first time at 14,
And spent most of my school holidays from that point on

In a children's psych hospital.
Now that's pretty **crazy**.

I wish I'd known I was **trans** sooner.
Everyone is impressed I came out so young,
Right before I turned 16,
But it didn't feel like the right time.
It felt astronomically too late.
I made so many choices up to that point to hide I was **trans**
That I wasn't even sure I knew how to be who I really was,
But I carved my new life with my new name,
And said fuck you to anyone who questioned me.
Now that's pretty **trans**.

My life has been surrounded by being
Blak, **broke**, **crazy**, and **trans**,
But the more I think about it,
The more I am proud it makes me, me.

Legacy

by KJ Hepworth

Creator Bio

Dr KJ Hepworth is a settler coloniser, writer, designer and researcher living and working on unceded Ngarrindjeri Land. Their disability justice-led, transmedia work surfaces how power intertwines data, functional capacity, kinship, knowledge traditions, and visual cultures. Known for exploring these intersections in zines and public speaking, their expansive creative production includes ephemeral and installation art, zines, poetry, data visualisation, explainers, moving image, and augmentative communication devices.

Dr Hepworth's work opens up relational, somatic, and tactile experiences that transmute the tension between inherited creative and destructive experiences of power. Disability, gender, hearing and sexuality marginalisations inform how their work centres access, reciprocity, and solidarity. Central themes of this work are co-creating emancipatory visions of the future, and designing accessible tools to step toward them.

Artist Statement

'Legacy' is about reclaiming disabled lineage. It was written during the early heights of the COVID-19 pandemic, when disabled people were being more blatantly and callously discarded than usual. In this poem, I draw strength from disabled family past and present, to support their endurance during that time.

Legacy

I'm looking for the stories
flowing through my family
into my sinews, and my veins, and my blood
I'm looking for the untold stories
Searching for an answer
To appease the rage inside my guts

Because the family stories live in me
And they're burning parts of me they hate
They're whispering
That I'll lose
everything
That none of this is real
They say I need someone to ignore
They whisper: Careful what you feel.

Because life is leaving, and being left
And working as much
And as hard
As you can
And you're better off
Keeping a safe distance
They say: Love needs a backup plan.

I'm the simmering family anger
At deprivation
And deceit
And hurt pride
The constant effort of forgetting
And I'm all the convenient lies

I'm great-old, tent-bound Uncle Jack
A hermit and recluse
After abandoning his two wives
I'm alcoholic Aunty Lorna's pain
I'm her sisters' grief
And I'm her son, permanently hospitalised

I'm Uncle Geoffrey, standing silent
Witnessing his dad's betrayal
I'm also his resolve to thrive
And the witness to him fail

I'm my father's genius
and his distance
I'm the loneliness that creeps
into the hearts
Of those he loves
While he continues on, asleep

I'm my abusers
And their abuse
and their fear, and pain, and shame
I'm their self-loathing
Wrapped inside self-pity
I'm their thunder, and their rain

These stories burn, they whisper, they feast on me
They're feasting on my essence
They grow big, and fat, while I grow too thin
eat their fill, and then
They burp, and grin maliciously
and wipe my essence off their chin

I'm looking for the stories
flowing through my family
into my fears, and my bones, and my mind
I'm looking for the secret stories
Feasting on my hunger
Bracing... for what else there is to find

Hurt

by Sally Ann Hunter

CREATOR BIO

Sally Ann Hunter was a biologist and environmental policy officer (BSc [Biol], MEnv Sts.) and is now a writer and poet. She has published a collection of poetry called *The Structure of Light* and a biography called *You Can't Keep a Good Man Down: from Parkinson's to a new life with Deep Brain Stimulation.* A paper she wrote on the biography was read on ABC Radio's *Ockham's Razor,* as was a paper on living with solar power. She completed a ten-month course called Manuscript Incubator through Writers SA. Also through Writers SA, she participated in Poetry Studio on Zoom with Jill Jones over several months. Her novel called *Transfigured Sea* (Nature Writing) was published in 2022 and another called *Golden Cups* (Historical Fiction) is in the process of publisher's revision. A number of her poems have been published in anthologies and online. She lives in the Adelaide Hills where she gains inspiration for much of her Nature Writing.

Artist Statement

This poem was written in 2023, during a poetry session run by Lindy Warrell.

Date rape is probably quite common in the history of women in my age group, living in Adelaide. As we were mostly quiet and submissive in those pre-feminism days, we didn't take any retaliatory action at the time. I didn't even know that such a thing as date rape existed. Even when it happened to me. I didn't tell anybody, and I only thought of it as 'that awful thing'.

Hurt

Why not be depressed?
                        There is reason
He took your body
                        Your personal space
He inserted his need
                        In your privacy

Heaviness lay on you
                        Like his body in the car
You couldn't move
Like a spider pinned through its flesh

But this time
                You are in your kitchen
And
     It's forty years later

Not only have you got major depression
But you don't know why

Overwhelmed by anguish
You can't see the future
                        Or even the present
And the past is horrific

attn: the ivory tower

by Victoria Knight

Creator Bio

Victoria Knight is a white, fat, queer, disabled researcher and creative type living on Kaurna Land. They are a PhD candidate in cultural studies, researching the intersections between fat and queer lived experiences. Outside of academia, they are a writer and occasional performer. Spanning the breadth of their research and creative pursuits is a commitment to fat and queer liberation, and the indelible influence of their own lived experiences with mental illness and neurodivergence.

Artist Statement

This poem is something of a sojourn through my experiences in academia as a fat, queer, mentally ill, and neurodivergent person. The opening of the poem is inspired by a piece of feedback I got some years ago now, querying the existence of fat studies, a field which has existed for well over twenty years which I focus on in my work. This particular incident is really symptomatic of how I have felt in academia—I am often made to feel as if I am too unusual, too difficult or too unequipped to deal with the field. I wrote this poem from those feelings.

There are so many barriers for marginalised folks in academia, too many to cover in just one piece of writing. With 'attn: the ivory tower', I wanted to speak to the feelings I carry around my own experiences in the hopes that they might resonate with fellow fledgling academics or with those already established who might seek to make things easier for their marginalised students.

attn: the ivory tower

'i don't know if that's a thing—*fat*
studies', they say before they search it, because it's a *queer*
sort of thing, a discipline that sends *'real'* scholars mad
because surely, it's nothing more than a lazy
rebuttal to the universal knowledge that you should focus
on shrinking your body to make it normal.

i know the way i work isn't normal,
as my gaze sits far across the room, pupils fat
and distant, not a semblance of focus
to be found even through the ballast of queer
scholarly solidarity. i know they think i am lazy;
i think it enough myself that it's hard to be mad.

in a way it was easier when i was just a little mad,
because in academia, we can pretend it's normal
if you're too sad to shower, but lazy? oh, lazy
we cannot abide, because allowing that will rather queer
the whole charade, my dear, and expose the big fat
fact that needs which diverge too far do not command our focus.

every day, i try so desperately to focus
on the work that i love. i am ceaselessly mad
when my brain can do nothing more than chew the fat
with people who get to go home and be normal,
with scholars who don't want to hear about my sad, mad, queer
little life, who have already deemed me too lazy.

it's very easy to tell someone that they're lazy
or distractable, or that all they need is to focus

when you don't live inside a brain that does its best to queer
every pitch, even the ones that you're absolutely mad
for. it's easy when you live inside a brain that's normal,
when your chance at normal has not grown forever fat.

so, i land here—there is no way to normal for my fat
queer mad self, and it's disingenuous, perhaps even lazy
to think that a comfortable home within academia's normal
was one i would ever make. i cannot, and do not want to focus
my way out of my own brain—to think i ever could might be mad,
might risk erasing the beautiful—the mad, the fat, the queer.

i hope i never strive for normal. i hope i let myself stay fat.
i hope every thought i have is queer. i hope i care less about lazy.
i hope i am loved while i focus. i hope i'm loved while i'm mad.

Messy Minds Are Magical

by Fig Kershaw

Creator Bio

Hi there from Fig Kershaw. Fig's pronouns are he or they. They're physically disabled and use a wheelie walker and an ostomy bag. They're also mentally ill with schizoaffective disorder and autism.

Basically, his body be broken and they hear voices. It's all part of the Figgy package!

They've learned to embrace their vulnerabilities and struggles as everyone should. Unfortunately, disableds and neurodivergent peeps are taught shame and told they need fixing instead of working with what they're given.

He loves creating body inclusive art. He makes colouring books and sell them at local art markets. Everyone should see themselves in art.

Artist Statement

My piece is about the chaotic beauty of neurodiversity. Sometimes my brain just feels full. Full of special interests, full of romantic thoughts, full of frustration or sometimes just full. If I could release some pressure, what would come out?

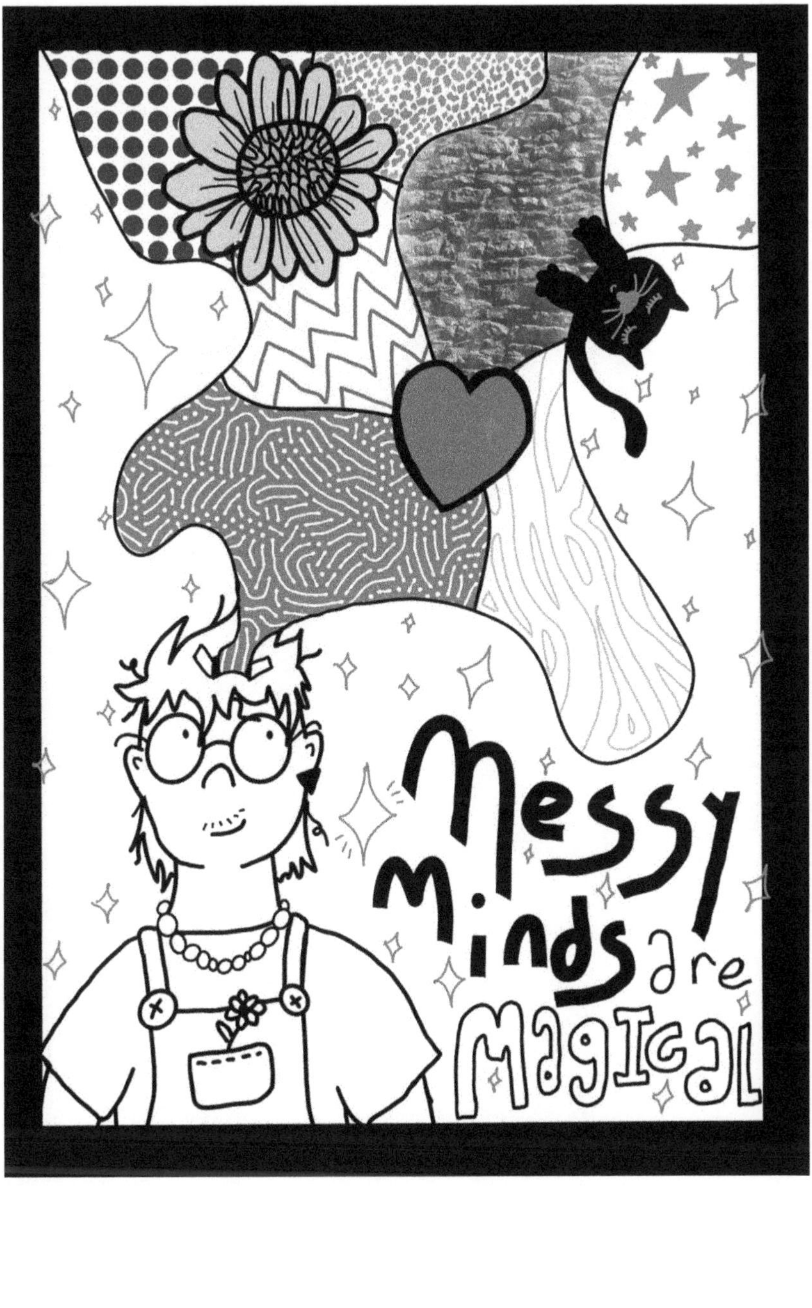
Messy Minds are Magical

Summer Cut
~
Send
~
The Extinction of Boys

by Cameron Rutherford

Creator Bio

Cameron Rutherford is a speculative fiction writer and the owner of Reed and Storm Editing, through which they provide editing services and sensitivity reading primarily for emerging authors and small publishers, and run creative writing workshops. They were previously a sub editor and frequent contributor to the Empire Times magazine. They have completed a Bachelor of Creative Arts (Creative Writing) with Honours, their thesis specialising in speculative fiction and constructed languages. Cameron's short story 'The Culinarian' was in the top ten shortlist for the Best Australian Yarn 2023 and was featured in The West Australian. Cameron's short story 'The Art of Robotic Burger Flipping' was featured in the Voiceworks issue *Static*. Their short story 'The Extinction of Boys' was highly commended in the 2022 Writers SA and Feast Festival Short Story Competition.

Artist Statement

Summer Cut and *Send*

I've never thought of myself as a poet. In my mind, these pieces are micro fiction with extra spacing. Regardless of what you call it, I feel the medium captures little moments well, and draws out implications of a bigger picture.

These pieces are about queer joy.

Summer Cut is inspired by haircuts given to me over the years by a housemate, a fellow queer nonbinary person. Most trans people can relate to the gender euphoria of a really good haircut, and that feeling is tenfold when the experience is given to you by someone who knows the feeling well and sees you wholly as yourself. This piece is a celebration of community, the spaces queer people carve out together and the euphoria that brings.

Send is inspired by the nerve-wracking moment of coming out. I've always found it difficult to come out in person, even with people I know will accept me. The words just won't come and anxiety hits me like a brick wall. Some people view coming out via technology less intimate, but to me the moment can be just as beautiful, just as tangible.

Summer Cut

The dining chair is dragged into the cosy bathroom.
You sit, surrounded by bright green plants,
growing in awkward directions.
The buzz cutter drones mechanically by your ear.
A white noise machine.
You feel your eyes closing.
The razor edge hums against your skin.
You feel the pressure of the hand behind it,
the faint sharpness of the blade,
and the touch is comforting, firm,
like the hand that holds your head steady in place
and tilts it gentle and apologetic.
You laugh warmly together.
The stray strands are cut loose
with slow deliberate clips
from a pair of old sewing scissors
that shines in the mirror's reflection.
They rustle loose ends from your shorn head
and you are yourself again.
You nap in the sun,
feeling less afraid of mirrors.

Send

You blink your eyes and rub them hard.
The lines of scrutinised words can't quite capture it.
You sit on your bed,
Phone cradled in your hands,
Still,
but your stomach is rolling.
You hit send.
Your head drifts to a cold future.
Your phone shines,
Warm in your hands.
A response.
I love you.

Artist Statement

The Extinction of Boys

Over time, the human Y chromosome has been shrinking and may one day disappear entirely. Many scientists believe the information held within the Y chromosome may be encoded onto another, but there are other ways humanity may work around this issue. In other species, including molluscs, true hermaphrodism occurs, meaning any individual can be impregnated and impregnate another. In some species, childbearing individuals can birth clones of themselves if no impregnators are around, a process known as parthenogenesis, including the New Mexico Whiptail which only contains childbearing individuals and are colloquially known as Lesbian Lizards, as intimacy between individuals stimulates ovulation.

I wondered how attitudes to sex and gender would change under these circumstances, especially as the process would take millions of years. Surely these social constructs would change to a point of unrecognisability, as humans themselves become unrecognisable, evolving to suit life beyond Earth. However, history and culture can be cyclical, so I envisioned a world where humanity returns to 21st Century gender roles due to the sensationalisation of the loss of the Y chromosome. Which sparked the question, what would happen if the last boy in the universe wasn't actually a boy?

The Extinction of Boys

Disclaimer: This story has been translated into 21st century English from 4th millennium Standard Martian by The Translation and Linguistic Evolution Sector of the Universal Time Traveller's Guild for educational purposes only. This document should under no circumstances be distributed to persons extant prior to the 4th millennium in order to prevent time continuum anomalies.

*

'And when did you know?' asked the holo presenter. 'That he was going to be a boy?'

'Well,' started Mumma, looking with a smile to Mother as she bounced baby me on her knee. 'When we found out Nova was pregnant, we went for the usual check-up, to see if there were any dangerous mutations in the egg and to do the usual modifications to ensure diversity in the human gene pool and all that. You've seen the PSAs.' Mumma rolled her eyes to the audience and they laughed. The appeal of being broadcast to every human colony in the galaxy hadn't worn off for her yet. 'But imagine our surprise when the doctor starts screaming for her co-workers to get in the room with us to check she wasn't seeing things!'

'Yes, it seems no one thought it possible for another boy to be born. Do you think there's any chance you two will one day have a grandson?'

'Well, the experts were surprised because they didn't realise the Y chromosome had been passed down in the first place,' said Mother seriously. 'I only realised at that appointment that I am intersex and have XXY chromosomes. When my father died eleven years ago the world thought that because he didn't have a son, he would be the last man in the universe.'

'But now the professionals have the whole picture,' said Mumma. 'Even if Orion one day becomes a father his Y chromosome is too small to affect his children, as my wife's own Y chromosome barely affected her.'

'So, we really are looking at the last boy in the universe?'

'That's right,' said Mumma proudly, shaking one of my chubby little arms at the camera.

'Why are you watching this?'

I turned to present-day Mumma, haloed by the permanently dusk-lit swirling clouds of Jupiter outside our living room window. She waved her hands through the holo projection as she took out the old tape.

'I found it while cleaning. I haven't watched the old interviews in a while,' I said, trying to distract myself by picking at a fingernail as Mumma chucked the tape aside with a crunch that made me wince.

'Come on. It's your mother's first day back from the True Human Society conference. You're having breakfast with us.'

We used to go with Mother to the big True Human Society conference on Mars every year, but Mumma grew sick to death of the things, a microcosm of the planet's bustling crowds and prying eyes. Now Mumma preferred to never leave the wealthy floating city of Jupiter we moved to for her sake, and frankly neither did I.

Mother was in the glass-floored kitchen, already eating and reading from a tablet on the island counter. 'Morning,' she said, glancing up.

I sat at the other end of the counter and Mumma served up our plates. 'How was the conference?' I asked.

Mother sighed. 'Controversial as always. They're never going to stop fighting over if genetic restoration or minimal interference is best. Let's not talk about work. What'd you get up to while I was away?'

I shuffled in my seat. 'You know, school, VR. I found out about this in-person social group that might be interesting.'

Mumma cocked her head at me. 'You haven't mentioned that.'

'Well.' I fiddled with the food on my plate. 'I know what you think about trans men.'

Mother blinked at me. 'It's a transgender group? Why would you want to go to that?'

'So—'

'Do you realise how much bad press we would get if you did that?' Mother pinched the bridge of her nose. 'People like that— It goes against what the True Human Society, what *our family* believes. You and your grandfather are the last men in the universe, and that can't be true if you believe what those people say about themselves. It's not that they don't deserve—'

'Nova,' said Mumma. 'Have you considered he might be lonely?'

Mother clamped her mouth shut and folded her hands. 'Well—'

'Orion is the only boy in existence. You don't think he'd want to spend some time with people who are at least a little bit like him?'

Mother opened her mouth to speak but nothing came out.

'Am I on the right track, Orion? Is that why you want to go to something like that?'

I nodded. 'Yeah, I think so.'

The room grew loud with the sounds of chewing and tools scraping on plates.

'Okay, Rae,' said Mother finally. 'Where is the thing, Orion?'

'Titan,' I said.

Mother groaned. '*Titan.*'

*

Titan, Saturn's largest moon, was more densely packed than even the biggest Mars colony, being a stopover point for asteroid miners and deep space travellers. The underground city was dark but filled with neon embellished life.

My flight had landed just minutes before and I felt lightheaded from the shift between artificial gravities. I wanted to explore the mix of cultures and cuisines and music and fashion in the streets but I trudged with my head down and hood up to the address I was given. I couldn't be seen here and, given my sheltered upbringing, I knew I'd stand out amongst the locals.

I slipped through the little door, looked around the poorly lit room.

'Hey! Orion, right? I'm Samson. We spoke in the VR drop-in space,' came a voice too close to me.

I turned to Samson beside me. He looked quite different IRL, but surprisingly like he had some True Human family.

'Come sit with us. We're about to start. Everyone's very excited to meet you. Obviously, they've never met a cis guy before.'

I followed Samson to the circle of chairs set up in the middle of the room. We went around, everyone introducing themselves. It seemed a pretty even split between trans men and nonbinary folk, pronouns varying wildly depending mostly on folks' first languages.

This place really was the True Human Society's nightmare. There were Mars natives, not people like my family who were born on Mars but bred specifically to retain traditional human features, but proper working-class locals with broad stocky features from their dense bones and dark, almost orange skin to protect from Mars' thin atmosphere. Then there were the kids of asteroid miners and deep space flyers, tall and thin from growing up with low-grav, their heads nearly touching the ceiling, pale like bone from lack of real sunlight. I was used to seeing moon folk at least, features not quite as exaggerated as the spaceflight kids.

The strangest attendee was the robot. Flesh-and-bone humans and the uploaded digital transhumanists rarely interacted, even within VR spaces. Being uploaded does something to the way you think.

I think he noticed my confused look as he introduced himself.

His chassis shook as he laughed. 'I know what you're thinking. Being trans is seen as a very physical thing. I can change my appearance to anything I like in digital space, or have no appearance at all, right? Different as we are from you corporeals, your culture bleeds into ours, especially the more new people get uploaded. For generations now 'woman' has been the default which causes a lot of social dysphoria for folks like me who don't fit into that category.'

'And that's relatively new as far as human history is concerned,' said a particularly short Martian. 'For millennia most human societies have been genderless, especially since parthenogenetic births started happening and "biological sex" became a whole lot less important as far as starting a family is concerned. It's only been since the sensationalising of the extinction of the Y chromosome that this obsession with the gender binary has started up again. No offense.' They shot a glance at me.

'No, you're right,' I said. 'But millennia? Trans people were accepted that long ago? Surely society hasn't regressed that much?'

'It's true,' said Samson. 'Our archives have some *really* old photos if you want to see.'

Samson passed me his tablet. I stared into the screen.

It *was* an old photo. Early first millennium old. The people in this trans support group looked very different from those in front of me. *They* were True Humans. Their heads were tiny, and their eyes were small as pin pricks. When they smiled their mouths were crowded and sharp. They were short and stocky and square. And their hands didn't look right. They looked more animal than human. But there they were, in clothes and buildings and machines.

I flicked through the folder. There were some holo restorations but most of the images were flat, 2D and dull. The videos moved jaggedly and the resolution was terrible. In almost every photo, they were laughing together.

Samson leaned over to point at a figure. 'That's one of our lost sisters. A trans woman.'

I looked into her eyes, smiling at the edges. The old humans didn't seem all too different.

*

Mother and I materialised in the virtual green room, waiting for the VR interview to start.

'What is your avatar wearing?' said Mother.

'What?' I said, looking down at myself.

'What happened to all the custom-made traditional men's outfits we had specially ordered for you?'

'This model is masculine. It's really popular with the guys from the group.'

Mother scoffed. 'Because they can't afford anything that's not storebought.'

A countdown timer appeared in front of us.

'Well, you don't have time to for a new model to load in now.' Mother sighed. 'Good luck, honey.'

I studied Mother's avatar for a moment. It was the highest quality you could get. It was like looking into her real face. As a parthenogenic birth I should have been a perfect copy of her. In the interviews her and Mumma always said it was a natural mutation that I didn't have XXY chromosomes like her, that I dropped the extra X chromosome and became the last boy. Sometimes I wondered if they removed it on purpose. I wondered how different my life would be if I was born like Mother. How much easier.

'Thanks,' I said.

I was ported to the interview space. All at once everything was loud and bright and colourful. The interviewer gave her over the top introduction to the virtual audience. I spied Mother and Mumma. I tried to smile, hold myself how I'd been taught.

'Now, let's get right to it,' said the interviewer, turning to me suddenly. I jumped a little. 'Can you explain these photos of you in

Titan heading to the location of an interplanetary youth transgender support group?'

An image flashed before me. Fuck. It was me sure enough. I'd been less careful about watching for paparazzi each time I went back to Titan. Mother and Mumma tensed in the audience.

'Yeah,' I said, trying to sound casual, like I hadn't just had my privacy ripped away from me by a professional stalker. 'I've been going for a while now. It's nice to be able to talk with other guys.'

'So you believe they are men? Doesn't that go against the beliefs of the True Human Society, which your family is part of? Against the idea of you being the last boy?'

'Well,' I started. The folks from the group were definitely watching. But so was the universe. 'Obviously it's different, but we share a lot of the same struggles. The galaxy isn't built for me or trans men anymore.'

I knew I had toed the line well. Too open-minded for most of the True Human Society, but not progressive enough to stand out to general audiences, though who knew how social media would twist my words. I didn't say anything of substance really, yet maybe I would help change some minds.

But still, I felt sick to my stomach.

*

Now the media knew about me going to the trans group, Mother and Mumma finally let me invite Samson over.

It was nice to relive the excitement of seeing the floating Jupiter settlement for the first time through his eyes. After a wide-eyed tour, we settled into the living room to mock the ridiculous things said in the old interviews and news stories about me.

My gut was sore from laughing when Samson went quiet.

'Ori, I'm sorry about the interview by the way. Maybe we should have moved the IRL meetings to Jupiter,' said Samson.

'It's fine. I know most people can't afford the flight here and someone was bound to notice eventually. Even if I kept to the VR meetings, my VPN and alt accounts get doxed all the time.'

Samson gave a big lopsided smile. 'So you don't mind being associated with us?'

'Course not,' I said, looking away to pick at a fingernail. 'I mind that people talk shit about you.'

Samson shrugged. 'We're pretty tough, and things are making a turn for the better.'

It was my turn to go real quiet. I shut of the holo player.

'Samson.'

'Yeah?'

'I think I'm a girl.'

Samson smiled slow. 'I'm glad you figured that out.'

My racing heart skipped a beat. 'You knew?'

Samson rolled his eyes. 'I mean, I didn't want to assume and you can't tell someone that before they're ready to say it themselves but… I've never heard of one of those assigned-male-at-traditional-birth True Humans associating with the trans community before. Not ever.'

I leaned back into the couch, let out the tension I'd been holding in my body with a slow exhale.

'In my experience, people who get invested with the trans community like you did are rarely cis. I felt a familiarity with you since the day we met, but not because we have manhood in common, or whatever. It's because you also know what it's like to be happier outside the role you were given.'

I felt my lower lip wobble and opened my arms wide. We hugged tight. 'Same here,' I said with a tearful laugh.

After a long moment, Samson pulled away. 'Have you told your mums?'

'God, no!' I said, wiping my eyes with the backs of my hands. 'No one is gonna understand why the last boy in the universe wants to be a girl, least of all them.'

'I understand. The group understands.' Samson knocked my elbow roughly. 'And you are a girl.'

I rubbed my elbow. 'I know that, but they won't. There hasn't been a trans woman in so long. The whole galaxy is watching me. They have so many expectations for me. I don't know how to deal with ruining all of that. It's easier to play along.'

'You really think you can fake something so huge to the entire universe? How are you going to do that without pushing everyone away? Without pushing your own parents away?'

I looked down, my stomach swirling again. 'It's worked so far, mostly.'

*

We had come with Samson to wave him off at the space port and now Mother, Mumma and I were alone in the flyer. We sat with our knees almost touching, me sitting opposite my mums, waiting quietly for the flyer's AI to land us back home.

My legs bounced anxiously, my body knowing it was a perfect moment.

'I, um—' My words caught and my throat was thick. 'I have something to tell you and you're not gonna like it.'

Mother and Mumma's eyes went from vacant to filled with worry. 'What do you mean?' said Mumma.

I went to speak but suddenly I was crying and I couldn't fit any words between the sobs and my head was between my knees and Mumma was rubbing my back. They were trying to console me, trying to lift my head up to tell me they'd love me no matter what, that everything was gonna be okay but I didn't believe them.

The flyer settled into the docking station but no one made to leave. I took big shaky breaths, finally slowed my crying enough to get the words out.

'I don't wanna be the last boy. I'm trans. I'm a girl. I wanna use she/her pronouns. I want—'

Suddenly their arms were around me. I choked back more tears. I wanted to see their faces. I wanted to know why they were hugging me so tight. 'You're not mad?'

'Of course not!' said Mumma and they broke away. 'Who cares what everyone thinks? I want you to be happy!'

'Mother?' I turned to her and she was crying, silently but her lip was trembling like mine does. I'd never seen her cry before.

'I had no idea you felt like this. I—' Mother wiped her face, composed herself, but her voice still wobbled. 'My father loved us but he made me and my sisters feel like there was something wrong with us for not being the boys he wanted. The thought that I've made you feel the same way, that I put pressure on you to be something you can't. I'm— I'm sorry about what I've said about the trans group.'

I threw my arms around her, buried myself into her.

'I love you so much.'

*

It was my first in-person interview in a long time. Mother and Mumma's presence beside me calmed my nerves, as did Samson and the rest of the group sitting in the audience, waiting to cheer me on when I broke the news.

'I'm trans,' I said. It kept getting easier the more I said it.

'Oh, you're going to upload yourself?' said the bubbly clueless interviewer. 'How wonderful for the last boy to be around for future generations to—'

'No,' I said with a laugh and the wave of a hand. 'I'm not transhumanist. I'm transgender. I'm a girl.'

Now the interviewer was stumped for words.

'You shouldn't think of this as losing the last boy in the universe,' said Mother, poised. She was always good at interviews. 'My father was the last cis man, but there are plenty of boys in the universe. We have some in the audience with us today.'

Mother gestured to the audience and I heard Samson whoop. 'We love you, Ori!'

I covered my face with a hand to hide my laughter.

'The universe is just learning about what it had all along,' continued Mother, unfazed. 'Which is my beautiful daughter, the last true trans woman.'

sketches of the bodymind

By Theo Brown

CREATOR BIO

Theo is an Irish Autistic trans QueerCrip artist living, creating, and resting on Kaurna Land. Theo predominately works with pencil and paper, inspired by queer and disabled artists of the past and present. He is known for his portraits focused on community leaders, the beautiful faces of Queer and Disabled people, created to remember their power and impact on our stories. Theo spends his time resting his body-mind and building safer community spaces with a passion for abolition and land back.

Artist Statement

An A5 graphite drawing centring a portrait of Claude Cahun, an androgynous white person with mime-like makeup, surrounded by 'masks' of faces hanging down, one of which is vacant and obviously mask-like, the other heart shaped and warmer, but crying. There is an unfinished sketch of soursobs off to the right.

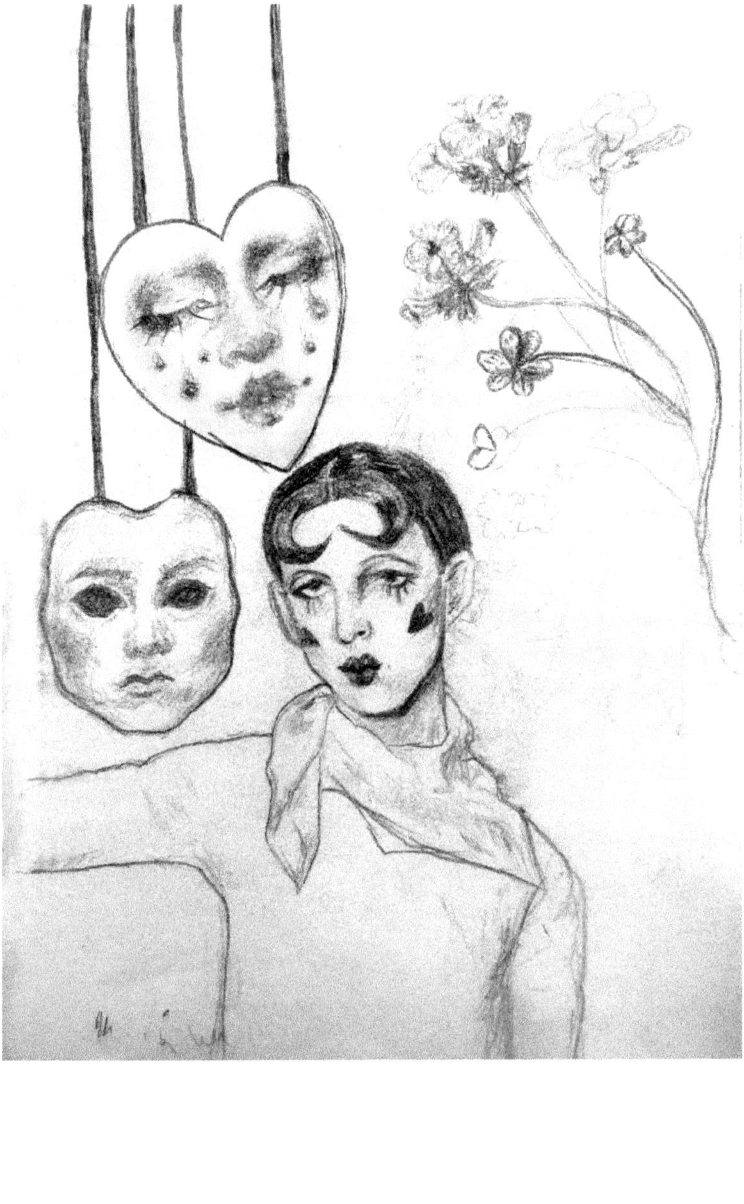

Artist Statement

An A5 graphite and highlighter drawing centring a portrait of Frida Kahlo sitting down and smiling contentedly, accompanied by a hand emerging from the bottom of the page holding up a flaming heart, with the text 'Sicko' cutting through the flames. To the left of Frida there is a sticker with the Palestinian flag and the words 'LAND BACK' in English and Arabic.

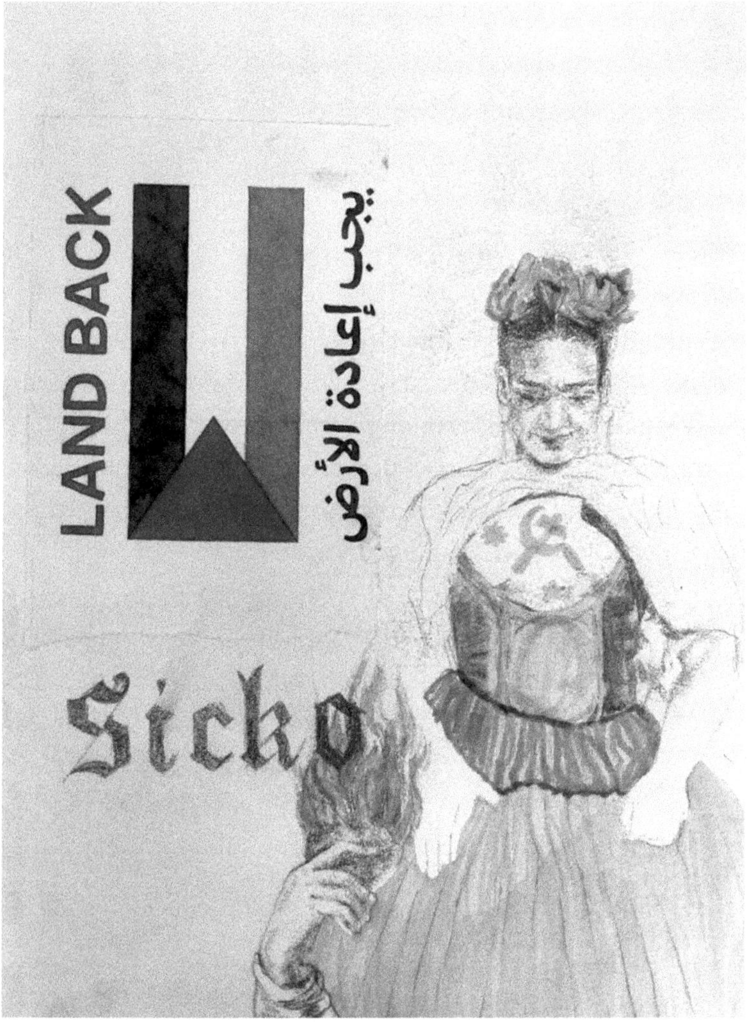
LAND BACK
يجب إعادة الأرض
Sicko

Artist Statement

An A5 graphite and Texta drawing of two portraits of Pedro Lemebel. In one he is looking intensely over his shoulder with a hammer and sickle painted on his face. In the other he wears a headpiece of syringes filled with fake blood that create a circular frame around his face. The Spanish text above the portraits reads 'un marica pobre y Viejo' meaning 'a poor old faggot'.

un marica pobre y viejo

Artist Statement

An A5 graphite drawing showing a hand cupping a burning flame within an ornate oval frame in the top left, and two sets of hands showing the two parts to the Auslan sign 'can't believe' below it.

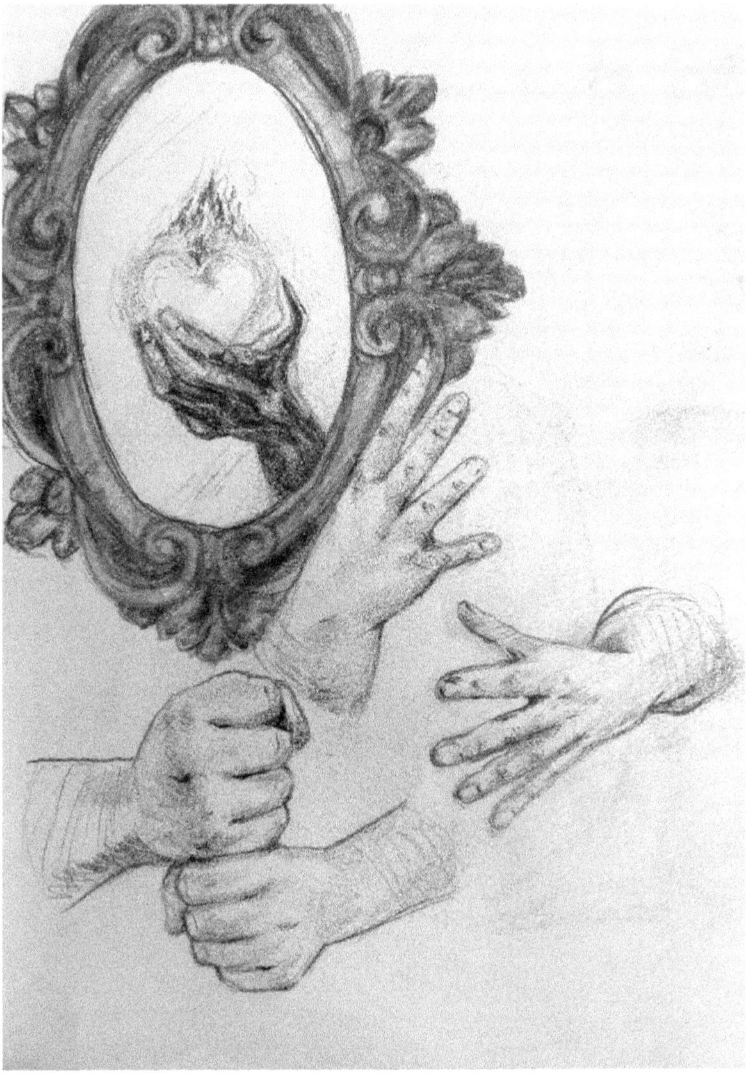

The Truest Letter I Ever Wrote

By Leon McAloney

CREATOR BIO

Leon McAloney is a queer, disabled artist who spends most of his time at the moment just resting. While he would love to spend all his time working on art and supporting all the artists he adores, he has had to take a lot of time for himself. Every now and then he'll emerge from his hermit hovel with four thousand words or some equivalent form of art showcasing the deeply personal, referring to his own experiences of disability, queerness, and trauma, before returning to another unspecified period of radio silence.

Artist Statement

'The Truest Letter I Ever Wrote' is a genuine draft of a letter I've been writing for several years to an important person in my life. While it may not resemble the finished product exactly (names and specifics have been altered to provide some ambiguity) this letter is the honest culmination of years of lying, putting oneself down, and the difficult relationship I knew inevitably had to end. I hope that sharing this deeply personal part of my process will assist others in their own healing journeys, at least to show them they're not alone.

The Truest Letter I Ever Wrote

I've thought about writing this letter for years. I think I was 19 when I thought about it for the first time. There were definitely more occasions where I wanted to communicate to you absolutely everything I hadn't been truthful about but New Years of 2019 was the first time I began thinking about this letter in particular. I didn't realise it at the time, but I wanted to tell you about my grief.

That day, I cancelled the plans I had to catch up with my friends so I could try to explain to you my side of our earlier argument. It didn't seem like a big deal at the time but maybe it was to you because when I tried to make up later that night, I was met with brutal remarks about how lazy, useless, and selfish I was. I was so shocked that I admitted the deepest kept secret I had—that if the way I had been living was 'normal' (as you had repeatedly told me it was) then I would have to kill myself. Your response was, 'You never think about anyone but yourself'. That was the first day I started actively grieving. Grieving 'us', I guess. The past I never got and the future I would never have.

I know that sounds dramatic but that's because it is. You always said you regretted getting me acting lessons as I was 'already dramatic enough'. I know you said it was just a joke (you said you were just joking a lot, even when you'd say the exact same things during our arguments) but I contribute those lessons to making this all much less dramatic than it could have been.

I was good at acting. I acted like I didn't think about everything you said every day. That your words didn't dictate every single thing I did and every relationship I ever had. Like I wasn't dying on the inside every time we met up. Like I wouldn't go home each time and cry. I wasn't *great* at acting. Anyone who stuck around with me long enough could easily see through the masks but it was enough for you.

At least, I think it was. It was enough when I lied to you about not being in the mental health ward. I didn't want to have to take care of you yet again while I was in some of the darkest places I'd ever been, specifically because of all this.

I'm going all over the place. Let me try again.

I want to tell you about my grief.

...

I used to think it was a grief for what we could have been. I know you wanted this relationship, 'ever since you were young' you used to say, and I know this in the way you hold on so tight even as I try to get away more and more. But we don't have that relationship, we never did, and we can't keep being whatever we are now either.

I needed you to do what you promised you would when you chose to take the role you did. I needed you to love me unconditionally. You couldn't do it. You needed me to take care of you and love you in a way that fixed everything. I certainly couldn't do that.

I'm not saying you don't love me. That would just be a lie and I will not lie to you anymore. I've done it way too much. I can't keep lying and putting myself down just for your comfort. I know you wanted me to—well, no, that's not really right—I think you wanted all the things I lied about to be true. It doesn't work like that. I couldn't just not be disabled, or forgive apologies I never received, and you didn't like it when I tried to explain that. So, while you probably didn't actively want me to lie, you certainly weren't okay with hearing the truth either.

Nonetheless, I was devastated to find out that your love was conditional. After all the years of hurting myself in order to meet those conditions, it took me a very long time to believe unconditional love was even real. Even when I found myself loving others unconditionally as proof, I started to believe maybe it was just me who wasn't able to be loved. Maybe there was something truly wrong with me and it was my fault your love didn't include all of me.

And that was when I started to think I was grieving myself.

The first time I admitted that, I drew upon a Hannah Gatsby quote I love so much:

> *When you soak a child in shame they cannot develop the neurological pathways that carry thoughts, you know, thoughts of self-worth. They can't do that. Self-hatred is only ever a seed planted from outside in. But when you do that to a child, it becomes a weed so thick, and it grows so fast, the child doesn't know any different. It becomes as natural as gravity.*

The second time I accepted I was grieving myself, I told the love of my life I didn't love myself. I told them I absolutely hated myself. It was true at the time and it often still is. We spent the evening, just the two of us, with her just holding me in his arms.

I used to think that I would eventually be able to just flip the switch of self-love, that one day something would properly click and I could finally get on without the constant flagellation I believed I deserved 24/7. It isn't like that obviously, but I didn't realise just how accurate Hannah's seed metaphor was.

You see, my self-hatred is within everything. Its roots are buried in every single memory and belief I have ever had. It isn't even as simple as 'I just hate everything about me'. I simply do not know how to think without it being coloured with the shame I feel just by existing.

I get angry at myself every time someone acts slightly different than usual. What else could the issue be but me, since I'm so terrible? I'm evil and selfish if I ever put myself first, even if it means forcing myself to be in more pain. I tell myself off if I breathe too loud, if I'm affected by my pain, if I am disabled by any of my disabilities, if I simply exist without constantly improving the lives of everyone within my orbit, even when I am completely alone.

And I can't be alone. Not without hearing that voice louder than ever. Too loud, too annoying, too weird, too selfish, even when no one is around to observe me. The voice made of those who were supposed to take care of me.

All of our thoughts and actions are based on memory, on past experiences, and my memories are of being made to believe I was lazy, selfish, and worthless. A burden. The more memories I made where my actions were based on these core ideas, the more they were fed and grown. Even now, after all this time of supposed growth and change, the feeling is reinforced by your words and your actions. Every thought, every action, every relationship I have, it's based on the only consistent data I've ever had—shame.

...

I'm going to take a minute to guess you're thinking, 'Well I didn't do all that! I didn't tell him to beat himself up constantly! That's ridiculous!' or maybe, 'Oh boo hoo, everyone thinks like that. You can't blame me for something everyone feels.'

I'll get back to the second thought but the thing is, you did do all that. You can blame your other half all you like (and you should, he is certainly not innocent) but you did this too. You can't keep pleading innocence when the tangible evidence is here, killing himself right in front of you.

What's worst of all, though, is you refuse to acknowledge it.

I'm not who I was as a teenager. I know I'm only four years out from being in my 'teen' years but I am so different to who I was. Trauma and healing from it can do that, I guess. For one, I don't think people are monsters just for making mistakes anymore. It took me a long time to learn that though, and not from being told to shut up and get over it if someone said slurs, funnily enough, but because others had the patience to let me make mistakes. They explained that, as long as I acknowledged it, apologised, and tried to do better, then guilt could do nothing more but remind me why I try to be better.

If you had acknowledged the mistakes you'd made, taken on your grief as your own, and tried not to repeat the past, I would never have written this letter. I could be honest with you and feel comfortable doing so. I would come to you when I was hurt and we would work it out, together, and I could stay to experience the new relationship we'd develop that would be so much stronger than what we ever had. I could actually trust you like you've told me I should so many times.

Instead, we have this letter.

Instead, my memories of you consist of me trying to be honest with how I felt and, instead of receiving any kind of apology, you making me responsible for your guilt and grief. I got told it wasn't as bad as I remembered, that my feelings were invalid or dramatic. I was told I was selfish for not caring about excuses when no apology preceded or followed them. I was told it was all just a mistake I should get over despite only being punished when I made mistakes.

I always knew you made mistakes and I don't think you should be punished for it either. I don't think you brushing aside my genuine pain, saying I was just 'seeking attention', was done with malicious intent. I don't think you planned for all of it to be compounded in my brain to the point I believed what I felt didn't matter. And, logically, if my feelings didn't matter, then clearly the person feeling them didn't either.

I have never thought for a moment that you wanted any of this damage but the hurt being caused by a mistake didn't change the fact it happened and that it continues to be reinforced each time you refuse to even acknowledge it.

I grieve that we will never fix the relationship I needed because when I came to you, telling you how your actions made me feel like I didn't matter, you continued to act the same. I continued to see my feelings were insignificant if it meant you had to put your own aside for even a moment.

So instead, you get a letter. A letter you could ignore as well but at least this time I won't ever have to know.

...

Even now, hours of therapy and thousands of words in, I find myself wanting to explain myself and apologise.

Even now, I feel bad for asking you to put my health over your hesitance to do the hard work on figuring out why you are so against what I need to do to live.

Even now, I want to write a thousand more words just to make sure you truly understand what I'm trying to say to you, so you can't misconstrue it.

But why should I do that? If you know me as well as you say you do, you would know I don't expect you to put yourself at a complete detriment for every single whim I have. You would know when I ask you to put yourself aside for a moment I want you to hold onto your guilt and grief and hear me out, rather than fight back because I made you feel guilty at all.

Maybe you would even know that I wish you didn't have to feel guilt, that I wish we had always had a perfect relationship like the one you pictured, where I wasn't disabled and you hadn't left me alone to deal with all the suffering. A relationship where you could take on the responsibility of your role and not make me take care of your emotional state at such a cost to myself.

I even still wish I wasn't this disabled or damaged so I could destroy myself just a little bit to fix everything you need fixed. Instead, I find myself slowly but painfully dying, mentally and physically, but not to fix anything.

I wonder if you'd say you don't expect me to fix everything for you. Maybe you truly don't but it's hard not to take it that way. You see, I know it's hard to help others when you yourself are so inundated with your own pain. I know it's hard to take on guilt or give what you promised when you're already struggling with your own emptiness and self-hatred. I also know seeds of self-hatred don't come from nowhere. They need to come from another fully grown plant.

...

So, the other night I was sitting in the backyard with the love of my life, smoking the cannabis I've been prescribed for the C-PTSD you don't know about and the Autism you do but barely. I was thinking about how, again, I had come home after a better than average catch up with you but was feeling absolutely terrible anyway. I was angry that I still regress to the constant self-hatred when I am around you and, for just a moment, I found myself thinking how maybe you're just a bad person.

That was stupid. It wasn't stupid of me to think it, I was processing, but it is a stupid thought. No one is unworthy of love, something I have repeated to myself more than I can count because I forget it about myself. I also know for a fact that you are wonderful.

I know for a fact how funny you can be and how much kindness you want to put in the world. How you have a lot of empathy, both for animals and people. How much effort you put into everything you do, even when you are drawing from an empty pool of energy to do so. But I also know that's not how I can perceive you, not with everything else entangled within it like endless roots of the saddest weed.

I feel like *that* 'you' is one that comes out so rarely these days that. In that moment, I almost forgot it all together.

So finally, following those stupid thoughts, I grieved for you. I grieved the sweetness that has always been present in you but was eventually overcome by the bitterness of the immense hurt you'd caused me. The longer others stayed the more they could see for themselves the things I had only told them about before—how your jokes stopped being funny as they became more and more self-depreciating, how frequently any criticism would be spoken over as you tried to explain you were 'trying really hard to do better', even though this was another example of the opposite.

I grieved the patience you said you have that I can't remember experiencing. You know I struggle with patience too. You've told me about it often but I don't think you realise why. I can't stand being 'patient' because I've only ever associated it with suffering. I'd have to be 'patient' when I was in pain because 'It's not that long' or 'It's not that bad'. Maybe that's why it was hard for you to be patient with me too.

I grieved the experiences you didn't get to have with me, even though that's what you would have loved the most. You never got to go out with me while I use my wheelchair, finally able to truly enjoy myself without being in endless pain. You didn't get to come to the first time I ever stood up and read my poetry to others, even though you took me to my first live poetry slam. I never could have invited you when I finally got to do it myself. That poem and every other after was about you.

A lot of my art is.

I grieve that you will probably never get to experience my art, experience the things I love because I don't yet know how to make art that isn't tainted by the years of constant shame.

Finally, I grieved you because I realised you didn't love yourself either, that you felt this shame too.

I think you're terrified of the guilt and how it could prove your shame to be right, prove that you truly are terrible and don't deserve love. I think you worry if people knew you, everything about you, they would stop caring about you. I think you even have proof that this could happen, that you are no longer loved because of how much you changed. I cried for so long that night because I realised you felt just like me.

...

I remember the years your knees cracked before you found a physio who was horrified no one had helped you before. I remember how often your shoulder ached, often enough that you would put a wheat bag on it even though you couldn't handle the heat just as much as I couldn't. I remember when you brushed off the hours you'd spend each night doing unpaid labour because 'they couldn't afford to pay' you for all that time and 'it just needs to happen'. I remember you being burnt out and burnt out and burnt out and burnt out. I remember every single time you told me you were scared to leave because 'who else would love me?' even when he clearly didn't. Not in the way you deserve.

Seeds come from an adult plant. A plant old enough to have its own system of roots. I believed that my pain, that my feelings, that I didn't matter because it was what you believed for yourself.

...

I think self-love is a habit. I say this because self-hate was a habit for me too. It was all I ever knew it, so it was what I always stuck to. But I've had more and more experiences with true unconditional love and I have kept reminding myself those memories are the ones I want to base my decisions on. The more I use these memories and the more I make myself act on the idea that I am loved and deserving of love, the less I will need to rely on these memories of self-hatred to inform my decisions. The more memories I make that are based on loving myself, the easier it will be to fall back on those memories instinctually. Habitually.

I hope one day you can fall into the habit of loving yourself too. It might take a while. It certainly will for me and I have half as many years of trauma to sift through, but I really truly believe you can and will thrive in your own self-love just as I will someday. One day, I hope I can see you, truly confident in knowing that the people around you want to be there because you are wonderful and loved like you deserve. I can't wait for you to be able to experience love without the fear of losing it if you show too much of yourself or make too many mistakes. I truly believe you will get all this and more because you are loveable. I love you.

I know this letter doesn't make it seem like that's the case but it is. It's why this hurts so much and why I desperately *don't* want to give you this letter. I have to though, I can't be around you while I work on this self-love for myself.

...

Right now, I need to reinforce my experiences with people who care about how I feel and want to make changes so I don't hurt anymore. I need to hold those who hurt me accountable so I can show myself I don't deserve to be hurt. I need to be around people who I can stand up to without fear of having their power over me abused in retribution. I need to let myself feel safe right now so I can teach myself what that feels like before attempting to be unsafe again.

And I don't feel safe with you. That's why I can't tell you this in person, that's why I can't come over even for a few hours, that's why I don't tell you anything important to me.

That's why I need to not see you anymore.

...

I guess that brings us to the end. An end? Of this letter at least. I still have so much to work on and even now I don't know the full scope of what that includes. But right now, I have realised something was wrong with our relationship and how much hurt I hold from it. I realised I was hurt because you were too but that I am not going to fix it for you. I grieved the relationship we'll never have and came all the way around only to realise that I still do. I think I always will.

I think that means I'm finally ready to end this letter. I'm ready to be honest with you, no matter how scared and devastated I am. I've accepted that this grief will probably always be a part of me and that it will always be a part of how I continue to interact with the world, but it won't always be as hard to deal with as it is now.

So, even though our relationship is ending after 25 years, I won't be. And neither will you. Maybe we'll be able to see each other again one far away day. We will be completely different and continuing to change but maybe, for the first time, we will honestly get to know each other.

    Truthfully not yours but with love,
    Leon

Pages of a Lifetime

by Freddie Foeng

CREATOR BIO

Freddie Foeng is a queer Asian-Australian artist that enjoys exploring the nuances of humanity through a range of expressions, favouring movement and words to convey their experiences in the world. Forever curious about identity, society, and how these influences shape our lives, they like to learn by exploring all the art forms they can. With firm roots in street dance, they are passionate about community and represent the Adelaide-based crew, Freak Nation. Primarily working on Kaurna Land, they were a part of the OzAsia CAAP Artist Lab in 2022 and 2023, and Music SA's Equaliser project in 2021. When they're not dancing or writing, you can find them at their day job, nose deep in a book, or dreaming about pastries and ice cream.

Artist Statement

It's difficult to settle on a permanent state of being. When you think you've found an identity that fits you, time passes, experiences shape you and the person you were is now a stranger. I go back in time to reflect on moments in my life where I've been at odds with my various cultures, identities, and personal views.

Spoken through advice given by well-meaning friends and family, I explore how these ideas about identity can be heavy with underlying themes of control, reflective of the beliefs we've been exposed to. While these can act as a source of comfort in knowing what's to come, they can also serve as a source of conflict when probed further. This poem helps me explore how I can find peace with my diverse and shifting identities. It asks the question: how can we take the meaning we want from our identities without needing to conform to the ideas that come with them?

Pages of a lifetime

Maybe if I read my diaries back,
I'd be shocked
And surprised
At how differently I thought
At different times of my life
When I think I've settled
On a state
I look back at my pages,
And see multiple 'me's
Processing life
Processing feelings
Processing being
How many different versions
Will exist while I am alive on this earth and in this time?
I surprise myself
With my changing identity
Forever adapting
To this changing world
And my changing internally
If I believed in past lives
Would it be easier
For me to remember
That I can be whoever I want to be
In this lifetime?
Growing up
Being perceived as a woman
And stuck in between cultures
Meant my strengths

Resided in my desirability
And simultaneous ability
To distance myself
From the feminine parts of me
I was conflicted and confused
Mum would say
Dad always wanted sons
So while you're beautiful
You don't really fit the bill
When you get married and have kids
You'll have satisfied the goals of your life
You'll go away
Follow your husband
And I'll be left alone
Because that's what we as Chinese do
And make sure you get married young,
So you have the best pick of men
Okay, I say
That's nice, Mum, but people tell me
You do what you want to do
Don't mind your family
This is a new generation and you are Australian
Women who are not like the others
Are the best kind
So be strong, be smart, defy stereotypes
But also be sexy, sweet and lean
So you can attract the One for you
I found happiness
In the fact that I was wanted
Masculine traits I had in abound
And I didn't really want to be a woman
So easy,
I could pretend to be a boy who looks like a woman

Deliver the best of both worlds
I couldn't satisfy my parents but at least I could
Fit the ideals of my society
I could change the way I was seen
Within the confines of the identities prescribed to me
Without realising that trading a square for a circle
Only meant I was changing shape and not my mentality
I followed the rules of life
And found success
But I struggled to fit the pieces of me
Through the holes that said
Now this will make you happy
Disappointing myself
Seemed to come with the territory
So maybe it's time I reconsidered
My relationship with this world
Look outside of what it means to be a woman or a man
Who exists for others
And start to embrace the qualities
That make me human
Woman and man
And the simple joys
I can find in living authentically
Following my desires
While being gentle, peaceful and loving
Words that will always describe me
Regardless of my shape or form
And words I will write again and again
In the pages of my diary

Milton Keynes UK
Ingram Content Group UK Ltd.
UKHW031140121124
451094UK00006B/582